BREAKING SHELLS

Neville Judson has had short stories, poems, stage and audio plays published and produced. He is a fellow of the Royal Society of Chemistry, and a keen caver and climber, which is reflected in the themes in *Breaking Shells*. He lives in rural North Yorkshire, between Harrogate and Skipton.

Breaking Shells

Neville Judson

LENDAL PRESS

First published in 2025 by Lendal Press
an imprint of Valley Press
Woodend, The Crescent, Scarborough, UK, YO11 2PW
valleypressuk.com

ISBN 978-1-915606-64-8
Cat. no. LP0023

A CIP record for this book is available from the British Library.

Cover and text design by Jamie McGarry.

Printed and bound in the UK by 4edge,
22 Eldon Way, Hockley, Essex, SS5 4AD.

I

'Come on,' shouted Simon. 'Dare yer ter climb over and stand on the wall where the water comes out.'

He was running with Ruth Hollingworth along a grassy path towards the sluice gates of a disused water mill, down the lane from Simon's house, on the edge of Church Wensley village in the East Midlands. It was 1957 and Simon had just passed his tenth birthday.

The four terraced houses on the lane – of which Simon's was the closest to the mill – were built from bricks of a bright, orange-red hue. When they caught the sunlight, it was as though they had taken on the glow of the kiln they had been baked in. The garden that sloped down to the lane from Simon's house was neatly kept, with marigolds and cornflowers on one side and runner beans, onions and lettuces on the other. A few scarlet flowers had formed on the runner beans and purple-tipped buds on lavender bushes that lined the path would open in a week or two, to release their fragrance.

Just beyond the mill, Ruth and Simon reached the sluice gates and stood looking at the supporting walls between the outflow slopes.

'Stood on them millions of times,' said Ruth. 'You haven't.'

'Dare yer, all the same.'

'No. I'm going down the field. Come on.'

'Cissy.'

Ruth ignored the insult, clambered over a wire fence, which twanged almost musically as her feet plucked at it, and started to wade through dock leaves that came up to her waist. Flecks of mud and green stains from the vegetation transferred onto her already grubby jeans. The duffle coat she was wearing had seen better times and now had worn patches around the elbows and an assortment of snags. Her besmirched clothing was out of keeping with her long, blond hair, which hung in neat plaits, but clean, smart clothes do not go with outdoor fun.

Simon followed with difficulty, being nearly two years younger than Ruth and not as tall as she was.

'Wait for me.'

As he jumped down, he felt a sharp sensation as a nettle brushed against his hand, but he gritted his teeth. He pulled off a piece of dock as he forced a passage through them, rubbing it on his throbbing skin until it was green.

Once clear of the docks, it was still hard to catch up with Ruth because the field had been made uneven by cows' hooves.

'Look, that's Lady's Smock,' said Ruth, slackening her pace a little and pointing at the delicate flower.

'Know it is, stupid,' Simon replied.

They ran to the confluence of the millrace and the stream from the sluice gates, splashed into the water almost up to the tops of their Wellingtons and started dredging for interesting things.

'Found a leech,' announced Ruth. She held up a stone and pointed at the writhing creature lying on it. 'If you get that on yer it'll suck all yer blood out, and you'll shrivel up and die.'

'Cor, bet yer dursn't touch it,' replied Simon, wide-eyed.

'Here – you,' said Ruth, holding the stone under his nose.

Simon backed away and plunged his hand into the cold water, eager to find something even more dramatic. He pulled out a handful of green slime full of little, wriggling things that reminded him of woodlice, and thrust them towards Ruth, who stepped forward to admire them.

'What about them then?' he asked. 'Will yer marry me when we grow up? I'm going to marry you.'

Ruth appraised Simon's marriage-worthiness. His wallflower-orange hair and hazel eyes were appealing but she was not sure that was enough. 'Don't be daft. My dad wun't let yer.'

'Why not?'

'I dunno. 'e jus' wun't.'

'Well, d'yer want to?'

'Dunno.'

'I'm not going to marry anybody if I can't marry you, 'cos I'm your lover.'

'Cissy.'

'No, I'm not.'

'It's cissy boys loving girls. Everybody knows that.'

'Well, I'm not cissy and *I'm* going to marry *you*, Ruth Hollingworth, so there.'

He plopped the slippery mass of weeds into Ruth's hands. Some of its inhabitants scampered for cover, while others ran halfway up Ruth's arms before losing their footing and falling into the water. She put the weeds onto a stone sticking out near the stream bank, wiped her hands on her jeans – transferring a faintly repulsive smell to them along with a new stain – and watched the frightened creatures scurrying down into the water.

A motorcycle was speeding down the lane and rounding the end of Simon's terrace. The sound carried with the wind across the field and Ruth looked up to see the motorcycle stop at the mill. Its leather-clad rider got off to open the gate.

'It's Jim,' she said. Jim lived in the house at the far end of the row from Simon's. He had just come home from work and driven straight down to the mill to look for Ruth. 'He's come to give me a ride on his bike. I'm going to ask him if I can go round the field on it like I did last week.'

'Can I have a go?' asked Simon.

'You're not big enough. You wouldn't be able to reach the ground with your feet. Anyway, Jim's my friend, not yours.'

'All right.'

The motorcyclist came through the mill gate into the field and rode down towards the children. They clambered out of the stream.

'Tra, Ruth,' said Simon, and he set off across the field, leaving Ruth to climb onto Jim's motorbike.

As Simon crossed the mill yard towards the houses, his friend from next door, Tim, came the other way.

'Ey up, youth, d'yer want to play by the waterfall?'

Simon came back with Tim, and they walked along the top of the retaining embankment that ran beyond the sluice gates. When Simon had come this way a few months previously on a stroll with his aunty, an angry swan had come out of the reeds and chased them away. The swans had left a while ago and there was no longer anything to fear. So the boys trotted happily on. The waterfall they wanted to watch was the overflow point for what remained of the mill pond, but someone had recently opened the sluices. The boys had never seen the water lowered before, and when they climbed over a stile beside the fall, they were dismayed to find that it had failed. They stood on the brink of the lip where the water should flow and peered into the deep pool below.

'If we make a dam the water won't ever be able to get out when it comes up again,' suggested Simon.

They started to collect stones and clods of earth and packed them in a narrow line across the top of the waterfall, glancing up at the nearby road bridge now and then to make sure no one was watching. They were making good progress, and were nearly finished, when Tim found out how treacherous the outer slope of the spillway was. One moment he was bent double, patting a wet lump of mud into shape between a brick end and a piece of old car tyre. The next moment, all that remained of him was the echo of a startled yelp.

Simon looked up from his labour of trying to pull a lump of broken concrete out of the ground and wondered for a moment where his friend had gone. Then the awful truth came to him. Tim was drowning in the bottomless chasm beneath the waterfall – or maybe being strangled by eels and eaten alive by giant pike. Should he run and try to pull Tim out of the water? He did not dare to, lest he meet the same fate, and he would surely not be able to reach down far enough even if he tried. He let out a howl, scrambled over the stile, and began to run back towards the row of houses where he lived.

It seemed a long way. One of his Wellington boots was full of water – he had not even noticed while he was dam-building – and the imbalance between his legs upset his running rhythm. At one point he was brought to a halt when a bramble took hold of his sleeve. He unhooked it, set off again and promptly fell over another one trailed across the path. But at last he staggered up the lane. He laboured, gasping, up the steep garden path to his house, ran round the back, crossed the yard and went through a little gate to the neighbouring house.

He banged on the door. 'Mrs Gregson, come quick – Tim's fallen in the river!'

Without waiting for a reaction, he returned to his own house and went in.

Everything was taking too long. Tim would be drowned and carried away even if he had escaped the onslaught of eels and pike.

'Mam! Mam! Tim's drowning in the river!'

Simon's mother came scurrying out of the kitchen with her hands covered in flour. She grabbed a long-handled broom and dashed out to join Mrs Gregson, who was hovering about in the yard. The three of them set off at a brisk trot, Mrs Farley trailing clouds of flour, Mrs Gregson hobbling along in one bedroom slipper and one heavy shoe. 'I was just getting ready to fetch Elizabeth from ballet,' she panted.

In the field on the other side of the mill, Ruth careered around at the controls of Jim's motorbike, but the rescue team did not even notice her. They hurried on between willow saplings along the curved embankment. The trees and scrub grew right up to the stile and so it came into view only when they were almost upon it. When it did appear, Tim – very wet and unhappy – was climbing over.

'Oh, thank goodness,' said Mrs Gregson.

Simon watched, strangely impressed, as Tim stepped off the stile and walked awkwardly towards his mother with his arms held out from his sides and with water streaming from his clothes. His tearful eyes were so blue they seemed to reflect the sky. His thin cotton shirt and shorts clung to his body and showed up every detail of it. Simon looked him up and down and somewhere deep inside himself he felt something that he did not understand.

2

Later that afternoon, the baggily-trousered nether end of Arthur Hollingworth was to be seen among the runner beans as he crouched on hands and knees with his head pressed to the ground. He was watching for his model train to complete its second circuit and race out of a tunnel he had built under the coal bunker. The circuit should then continue the long haul up a mound that had formerly been an unsuccessful attempt at a rockery garden and then part of a projected but abandoned crazy golf course.

The train did not turn up. It had most probably been derailed, and it would be lying in deep water at the edge of the fish pond again. When he looked into the pond though, all he saw were the three goldfish and a crown cap off a lemonade bottle that he had been meaning to get out for months. He looked harder and his puzzled reflection stared back at him.

He went through the side gate and hurried past the kitchen window. A landslide of nutty slack had crashed down from the coal bunker onto the train as it entered a cutting that led to the tunnel. He dug the train out and started to brush the dust off with his sleeve.

He had finished the carriage-cleaning and was about to start clearing the track when the kitchen window opened and his wife, Mary, stuck her head out.

'Arthur, tea's ready.'

He left the track clearing for later, carried the train to the rolling stock sheds, and went into the house.

'Arthur, your shoes! You're trailing coal dust everywhere!'

Arthur took off his shoes and put them on a sheet of newspaper just inside the back door before going to the kitchen sink to wash his hands.

'Where's Ruth?' asked Mary. 'I thought she was with you.'

'She hasn't come home yet. I think she went to play down by the mill.'

'That girl! She's never here when it comes to mealtimes.'

'I'll go and look for her.'

Arthur went through to the front door, stepped outside, then remembered he had taken his shoes off, just too late to stop the door latching behind him. He rattled the letterbox. The door opened a few inches and his wife's hand came out through the gap clutching his shoes. As the door clicked shut again, Ruth appeared at the gate.

'Hello, Dad. Why is your face so dirty?'

'Never mind my face – look at you. Where on earth have you been? You're covered in oil. Come on. We'd better get you cleaned up ready for tea.'

Arthur turned to go in, glowered at the closed front door, and then took Ruth by the hand and led her round to the back one. Once they were inside, he started stripping off the layers of swarf while Mary sat at the table and fussed about the delay to the meal.

'It's only salad,' Arthur observed. 'Surely that can't spoil by being kept a few more minutes.'

Eventually they got themselves settled at the table.

'Oh Lord, we thank thee for these and all thy manifold blessings,' Arthur intoned.

Mary promptly got up again.

'I think I'll get the trifle and put it on the table, to save having to fetch it when we're ready.'

She went into the pantry, took the trifle from the stone thrawl that ran along its far wall and set off back towards the table. When she got part way across the room, she turned away again and fetched a cake stand bearing a sturdy-looking fruit cake. She started towards the table but she was not to make the journey. Barely halfway, she tripped over a tumbled pile of back copies of National Geographic. The bowl of trifle sailed through the air and landed within an inch of the cat, jettisoning its contents over her and leaving a surprised tabby head protruding from the top of a pink and yellow pyramid. The cake came down on Ruth's clockwork train, rolling the locomotive onto its back. Shocked into action, its mechanism set its wheels spinning like the legs of a beetle trying to right itself.

'Thank goodness the cake got the train and not the cat,' thought Arthur.

3

One Saturday morning later in the year, when Simon came home from his weekly task of fetching the eggs from the top of the lane for his mother, his pockets were bulging. Most Saturdays he collected Tim from next door, once the job of collecting the eggs was out of the way, and they would set off on an escapade. October was a particularly good month for escapades because the village shop turned into a munitions depot in the run-up to November 5th.

Shelves in front of the counter that normally contained liquorice bootlaces, aniseed balls and humbugs were stocked instead with Brock's fireworks. Simon had extended his journey to spend the greater part of his pocket money on bangers.

He went next door and poked his head in. Tim was the mischief-maker when it came to confounding authority, but Simon was his ideal accomplice. He was the brave one when practical daring was called for.

'Come on, youth! Get yer bike!'

They pedalled up the hill from their homes, along the main road at the top, over a bridge and beyond until they came to a level crossing. Sometimes they would walk along the track from here to put stones on the rails, and then wait for a train to come along and crush them. The glassy remains had a strange, almost-metallic smell. On this occasion the gates were already closed and Tim and Simon waved to the train as it passed.

When the gates opened, the boys cycled on for about a mile before turning to go to a quarry up a stony road with rickety signs at its entrance declaring it to be private and dangerous – adjectives calculated to draw young adventurers from afar to investigate. Just out of sight of the main road was a big patch of brambles, behind which the boys hid their bicycles before creeping up the quarry road, keeping to the verge to be less conspicuous. They were unlikely to encounter enemy forces on a Saturday – the quarry no longer worked at weekends – but it was always wise to be cautious.

As they came round the corner of the crushing plant, there was a sudden noise of stones skittering against a corrugated iron fence at the back. The boys froze. A rabbit scurried out of the yard and disappeared into the undergrowth. Simon smiled and pretended to wipe his brow. Tim smiled back, holding his hand over his heart. He strode right across the middle of the yard to the foot of an inspection ladder, which he started to climb. Simon followed him up a series of these ladders until they stood at the very top of the plant and looked down onto the huge, rusty grading drum. The wind was cold in spite of the sunshine. Simon felt it and shivered.

From below the drum a wooden water channel ran across the roadway on trestles and then sloped down to a group of settling tanks. The tanks were full but the channel was dry. Simon climbed over a safety rail and lowered himself onto the drum.

'What d'yer think yer doing?' asked Tim.

Simon hooked one hand under the rail, let go with the other, turned and waved towards the water channel, lifting one foot at the same time to point in the same direction.

'I'm going across the bridge.'

'You can't do that. You'll fall off!'

'Na, I'll be awright.'

'Well, I'm not coming.'

After watching Tim clamber back down the ladders and run to the other side of the yard, to a place where he had a clear view of his friend, Simon waved his feet over the side of the drum, searching for something to step onto. One foot found a supporting strut and he swung over, looked down at Tim and then sidled along until he came to the water trough. Now that he was close to it, it did not look so secure. It was alarmingly narrow, not very deep, and a terribly long way off the ground, but he could not go back – climbing the rounded drum would be far too scary.

He summoned up the courage to take a couple of steps along the trough before deciding in favour of crouching in it, with a hand on each side, and shuffling along. The sloping section of the trough at the other end was a lot steeper than he had imagined and it looked very slippery. He poked one foot down the slope, then withdrew it and tried the other, but it did not feel any better. He sat on the edge of the slope with both feet over and eased himself forward. He found that he could maintain control by pushing his feet out sideways against the walls of the trough as well as using his hands to cling to the tops of them, and he began to slide down slowly.

Everything went well until he came to the bottom of the chute. As his feet slipped off the end, he shot forward and a plunge into the brown water seemed inevitable. He grabbed at one wall of the trough with both hands and stopped himself on the brink of disaster, letting just one foot dip into the water. He scrabbled for the side of the tank and managed to get his feet over it. Tim leaned across to reach Simon's arms and pulled him to safety. They sat on the sandy slope beside the tank and Simon held his leg in the air so that the water ran out of his shoe.

Tim pointed to Simon's hand. 'Cor, what's that?'

Simon looked at his hand and saw a splinter buried deep. The flesh around it was already blackening, and now that he was aware of it, the wound took on overriding importance and began to throb. Simon looked back and forth between his hand and Tim's anxious face.

''S awright. I've got my knife,' said Tim.

Simon's pulse raced in anticipation of major surgery without anaesthesia. 'It's got tweezers in it,' Tim continued.

This reassured Simon little, since he did not relish the idea of the splinter being plucked harshly from where it lay. In fact he began to think that the pain was not so bad after all and that he could be proud to live with the splinter embedded in his hand for ever, as proof of the brave stunt he had just completed. Tim was evidently set upon being cruel to be kind. He took his Swiss army knife out of his pocket and pulled out the little pair of tweezers.

'Give us yer 'and.'

Simon held his hand out.

'Don't look if you don't want. I'll tell yer when I'm gonna gerrit out.'

Simon concentrated on the neat cropping of Tim's black hair as he bowed his head over the site of the operation. He felt Tim probing gently and there were some sharp stabs of pain as he tested the grip of the tweezers on the splinter. Tim continued a steady patter of reassurance as he got ready to act in earnest, like a dentist getting a good purchase on an offending tooth.

Without the promised warning, he snatched the splinter clean out in one go. Simon yelped and then sucked at the bleeding hole at the base of his thumb while Tim sat with one arm round his shoulder and held up the prize for viewing with his free hand.

'Thanks, youth,' said Simon between suckings of blood. 'Be awright in a minute.'

A minute had barely passed before he stopped sucking his hand and jumped up. 'Come on. Let's blast the sand heap!'

They dashed off to the towering piles of sand and gravel. Simon pulled a banger out of his pocket and buried it right up to its fuse at the foot of a miniature cliff which he had just kicked into being. He took out his matches and lit the fuse, and the boys 'retired immediately', as the label on the firework quaintly advised. The banger hissed and roared, and then with a mighty crack it fired the remains of its case halfway across the yard and blew a great hole in the base of Simon's cliff. The sand pile thought about it for a moment and then a satisfying landslide commenced. The boys watched the last grains of sand come to a stop.

Simon set off to insert another banger, but Tim stopped him. He was holding a short section of copper pipe which he had found.

'Let's make a super bombshell out of this.'

They closed one end of the pipe with a piece of wet earth, sprinkled in a layer of sand, and then dismantled all but one of their remaining fireworks and poured the contents out of them into the tube. Simon cut off the base of the firework they'd put aside, inserted it into the pipe to act as the detonator, and packed it into place with sand and earth. They examined their creation and looked around for something worthy of its ferocious power.

'I know,' said Tim. 'Let's make it into a depth charge in the water tank.'

They went over to the tank at the bottom of the chute that Simon had come down.

'Here, I'll light it and you drop it in,' said Tim. 'Ready?'

'Yeah!'

Tim struck a match and lit the touch paper. Simon leapt to the side of the tank and threw the firework over, and the boys ran as hard as they could to the far side of the yard, expecting a tidal wave to burst through the wall of the tank.

Nothing happened.

They waited and waited, but still nothing happened.

After a few minutes Tim said, 'It's your fault. You threw it in too quick before it was going properly.'

'I wasn't going to get my hand blown off!'

'No, well, you should have waited longer.'

Simon got up from where they had been crouching behind a couple of oil drums and went across to the tank. He pulled himself up the side and peered into the muddy water. There was no sign of the bomb.

'I'm fed up. I'm going home.'

They walked back to their bicycles in silence and set off. When they got to the bridge over the brook, Simon dismounted and leaned with his chest against the parapet. Tim did the same, and they stared down over it.

'It wasn't my fault,' Simon started. 'I spent my pocket money for three weeks on those fireworks and it was all wasted because of you.'

'It wasn't my fault! You threw it in the water.'

'Yes, but it was your idea.'

'How did I know you'd let it go before it was burning?'

'I've had enough of you. I'm going to see Ruth.'

They got on their bicycles and set off in opposite directions – Simon towards Ruth Hollingworth's house, Tim towards home.

After he had gone about a hundred yards, Simon changed his mind. He turned round to pedal after Tim just as Tim turned back towards him. They met on the bridge, glanced at each other, dumped their bicycles, and went and stood against the parapet, gazing down at the brook again.

'We'll always be friends, won't we?' said Simon.

Tim gave the slightest nod. The boys looked into each other's faces, shook hands rather formally and cycled home together.

4

Arthur Hollingworth, confined to indoor activities by the darkness of an autumn evening, was building a model railway carriage on the kitchen table while his wife, Mary, bobbed up and down beside a loaded clothes horse, attending to the ironing at the other end of the room. The dilapidated ironing board was set at its highest level – the worn-out adjustment lever only locking into place at its maximum setting. It made her look even shorter and dumpier than she actually was.

Ruth was on the floor between her parents in front of a glowing fire, with a copy of *Reach for the Sky* hidden inside a translation of the *Odyssey*, which she was supposed to be reading for homework – it being considered appropriate classical education for twelve-year-olds. The air was full of the smells of the bubble and squeak they had eaten earlier, damp linen, solder flux and Arthur's charred fingernails.

There was a knock at the door and Mary went to answer it. Harold Prentice, the history and religious instruction teacher from the local grammar school, was standing on the doorstep in the pouring rain. Mary groaned inwardly but nevertheless gave Harold a welcoming smile and invited him in. He was a highly respected ley preacher and member of the local Baptist church that Mary and Arthur attended, and he was well-meaning, but Mary found his severe style of Christianity depressing and, though she hardly admitted it to herself, she found him physically repellent because he always reeked of tobacco.

'Come through and dry yourself by the fire,' she said, leading him into the kitchen. 'Arthur, it's Harold.'

Arthur looked up from his work, and the coupling that he had been soldering into place fell off and stuck to the back of his hand, burning a little hole in it. Mary returned to the ironing board, picked up the iron and slid the sheet on which she had been working swiftly towards her to pull the new, iron-shaped brown patch out of sight. Ruth closed her book as far as she could for fear that Harold would look over her shoulder.

He noticed the cover. 'Dawn comes with rosy fingers,' he observed.

Ruth looked at him blankly.

'Never mind,' he said. 'Arthur, I've come to make a proposal. Well, Mary may be interested to hear about it, too.

'I am concerned about the welfare of our youth – the young men of our church and community. I notice that they haven't enough to do and I think they should be occupied in character-building activities. Only yesterday, as I was going home from Bible Study Group at almost ten in the evening, I saw some youngsters still out on the street who could not have been more than fifteen.'

He turned to address Mary.

'Boys and girls together, Mrs Hollingworth. Their conversation was not entirely proper, and one of the boys had his arms round two of the girls' waists.'

He glanced briefly at Ruth, before finding his gaze settle on her sonic ray gun, which was lying on top of a stack of magazines in the corner of the room and pointing rather disconcertingly towards her.

'Our children face moral danger and we have a duty to provide them with Christian surroundings. If our children should fall prey to the ways of wickedness then it is we who must, at least in part, take the blame.

'Scouting for boys – I have always believed in it. I propose we start a troop in the village. A troop run by the church would be a training ground for manly soldiers of the Lord...'

'Can I join?' Ruth piped up. 'I've always wanted to be a Scout and climb trees and build bridges and play British Bulldog and...'

'Don't be silly, Ruth,' said Mary. 'Girls don't join the Scouts.'

'Why not, if they want to?'

Harold looked down at Ruth, sitting on the fender. 'Girls join the Girl Guides,' he explained. 'Boys join the Scouts and girls join the Girl Guides. They couldn't all go swimming and camping and doing things like that together.'

'Why not?' asked Ruth.

Harold coughed his smoker's cough and looked at Arthur. Arthur was searching for the coupling, which had fallen into a tin of washers when he brushed it off the back of his hand. Mary was crouching down over the clothes basket, getting the next item for ironing.

Harold looked back at Ruth. 'Well,' he began, looking rather flustered, 'there might not be enough tents for them to sleep or get changed in separately.'

Ruth did not say that she found it puzzling that this should matter, but Harold could see it in her eyes. How easy it would be to spoil her childish innocence with a careless word. He smiled and turned back to Arthur.

Arthur's mind had somehow wandered from Lord Baden-Powell to the relief of Mafeking, and onwards to a fearful journey with the young Churchill, hidden inside a goods wagon, steam-hauled across the High Veld. He had just jumped down an embankment and rolled under a bush, when everything went quiet and he rocketed back to the kitchen table too late to pick up his cue.

Fortunately, Mary remained alert as always, and spoke up from the prompt corner. 'You were in the Scouts, weren't you, Arthur?'

'I've still got the badges to prove it somewhere.'

The exchange, though unrehearsed, led Harold neatly into his next line. 'That's why I thought of you when the idea of a local troop came to me. I did a lot of Scouting myself before I moved from Nottingham. The fact is, I am not that good with the younger ones and I rather wondered if you would look after them. I'd be happier to take them on in a year or two when they are fifteen or sixteen – Venture Scouts – mountain walking and that kind of thing… unless you feel you would want to do that.'

Mary replied. 'I don't think Arthur could take lads up mountains. He won't even climb the loft ladder.'

Arthur much preferred the excitement of pretended adventure to the real thing, which had a tendency to get out of hand in his experience. Running a junior troop would suit him better, since it was sure to be made up of young enthusiasts for adventure fantasies.

'Yes,' he said. 'I think a Scout troop is a splendid idea. Venture Scouting really would not be my sort of thing, so if that is what you want to do…'

'I was sure you'd agree.'

Ruth had re-opened her books but her mind was not on either of them anymore. She was high on a sunbathed, limestone crag, looking down on rooks wheeling about the green mop-top of a tree in the valley below. She felt strong and brave, and most of all she felt free.

'I want to go climbing with Mr Prentice,' she muttered, staring at a cat flea poised on the carpet and preparing to leap onto his trouser leg. 'It's not fair.'

5

Ruth was naturally athletic and the determination that she put into excelling at sport over the next couple of years led her, by the time she was fourteen, to be running for the county in the National Cross-Country Final.

On her first day at grammar school she had decided that she was going to befriend the games mistress. She had not even known that Lena Goschalk was the games mistress when she made the decision, but it would not have mattered what Miss Goschalk taught. Whatever it was, was going to be Ruth's favourite subject. What so excited Ruth was Miss Goschalk's arrival at school, clad in leather and riding on a stupendously impressive motorcycle, which Ruth later learned was a rare thing called a Douglas Dragonfly. It had two cylinder heads sticking out sideways which made it look very grand, and when it went along, it produced a deep, satisfying purr that breathed effortless power.

Miss Goschalk's manner of dress and mode of transport appealed to Ruth because of what they said about her approach to life. Only eccentric adventurers like Ruth's great aunt, who had ridden across the desert on a camel to see a stone city called Petra, behaved like this. Ordinary women did not – were not supposed to. Mrs Gregson once described her aunt as 'behaving more like a man than a man'. Great Aunt Ethel was Ruth's kind of person and so was Miss Goschalk.

It was a happy coincidence that Miss Goschalk was the games mistress. Had she taught mathematics, Ruth would have had a hard time. She would have thrown herself wholeheartedly into trying to conquer calculus, but it is probable that calculus would have won in the end.

For the first part of the race she led the field, but she took care to pace herself, so that she only just held the position. There had been a lot of rain during the week and the going was heavy over paths recently ploughed up. The clay soil clung to her shoes until she felt as though she were running in steel toe-capped miner's boots.

She leapt into a ditch and scrambled up the other side into a little wood. Running was easier here because the ground was covered thickly with leaves that made a firm, padded surface. A girl cut past on another track through the undergrowth a few yards to one side and began to pull in front. Ruth tailed her, not trying to take the lead again yet.

When they came out of the wood and into a muddy lane, they had about a mile still to go – three quarters of it along the lane and then a final stretch across the school field and up a steep, grassy slope to the finishing line. The run along the slippery lane was tiring but at least the race had become a competition between only two people – the rest of the runners had dropped well behind. The gap in the hedge where they were meant to leave the lane was unclear and the other girl overshot it. Although she realised at once what she had done, it gave Ruth the opportunity she needed to overtake. But a few hawthorn roots twisted out of the eroded slope on the other side of the gap. Glancing over her shoulder, Ruth caught her toe against one and fell. Her opponent side-stepped past her and set off across the field with a satisfied smile.

Ruth wasted no time in getting up but another competitor in a bright blue tracksuit came out of nowhere and passed her. The two girls started to sprint, each determined not to be in third place. As they started on the steep, final slope, they saw something that made them fight even harder. The leader was flagging and they were gaining on her. At the top of the slope, with less than a hundred yards to go, they caught up with her, but the girl in blue moved ahead again. The erstwhile leader found new strength and the pace went up another notch but Ruth still managed to pass her and was only a foot behind the girl in blue.

They were almost at the finishing line when Ruth heard Lena Goschalk's voice from among the watching crowd.

'Go for it, Ruth! Go for it!'

Ruth made a final effort. The finishing tape snapped, and the race was over. She did not know who had won. She only knew her foot hurt a lot. As her pace slackened, she felt dizzy. She half lay down, half collapsed, rolled onto her back, and closed her eyes. The voices around her went distant and confused for a few seconds. When she opened her eyes, she was looking into Lena Goschalk's face.

'Well done, Ruth.'

'Was I first?'

'By inches.'

'My foot hurts.'

Ruth sat up and started to fiddle with her shoe lace.

'Leave it till we get to the changing rooms,' said Miss Goschalk. 'Come on – I'll give you a pull up.'

She hauled Ruth to her feet. Ruth put her hand on Miss Goschalk's shoulder, Miss Goschalk put an arm round Ruth's waist and they staggered to the changing rooms, where Ruth was deposited on a bench. Miss Goschalk knelt down and took her shoes off for her.

'Mind. It hurts,' complained Ruth.

'I'm not surprised,' said Miss Goschalk as she peeled off the left sock to reveal a bruised big toe and rapidly blackening toe nail. 'I think we'd better get you cleaned up and take you down to casualty to have it looked at. Can you hobble into the shower, or would you rather stay dirty?'

'I'll manage.'

Ruth shuffled into the shower with the other girls, watching their feet as they jostled to get at the water and keeping her toe out of the danger zone.

Miss Goschalk had arrived on site in the minibus. Another team member's father had brought Ruth with them in his car. So he agreed to take Ruth and Miss Goschalk to the hospital. There was hardly anybody waiting for attention in the casualty department and they were seen almost at once. The nurse explained what was going on while an X-ray was taken, but Ruth was not paying attention. Her preoccupation was with a promise Miss Goschalk had made that now seemed sure to be spoilt by the accident.

'I don't suppose we can go to the shops now.'

'I didn't think you'd want to bother – not with a broken toe.'

'It isn't broken. At least, we don't know till they get the X-ray back. Anyway, it doesn't matter if it is.'

'All right, if you're sure.'

When they got back to the car, Miss Goschalk spoke to the driver. 'Do you mind very much if we make a detour into town on the way back? I want to take Ruth there before the shops shut.'

They stopped at a shop full of motorcycle clothing and mechanical bits and pieces. When they came out, Ruth was clutching her first crash helmet – a gift from Miss Goschalk for winning the race. But this was only the beginning. Miss Goschalk had promised that once Ruth had a helmet, she would be allowed to ride pillion on the Douglas Dragonfly.

'Can we go for a ride on it now?'

'If Mr Yardley will drop us at my house, we'll get the bike out and I'll take you home on it.'

Ruth clapped her hands.

At the house, Miss Goschalk changed into her leathers, and they set off by a roundabout route to Ruth's. When they arrived at the garden gate, Ruth did the nearest thing that she could to jumping off and running to the front door with her sore toe. She rattled the letter box, but she did not need to because her father had seen her coming. He looked out and greeted Miss Goschalk, who was still with her motorcycle beside the gate.

'Won't you come in for a few minutes?'

'Thank you, but I must get back. I just wanted to see Ruth safely home.' She walked up the path to explain about Ruth's foot. Then Ruth and Arthur watched her start up the motorbike and ride off before they went inside.

'What has that girl got on her head?' exclaimed Mrs Hollingworth.

'It's my crash helmet,' Ruth replied. 'I got it for winning the final.'

'You won!' said Arthur. 'Well done.'

'What on earth do you want one of those for?' Mary Hollingworth asked.

'So I can ride on Miss Goschalk's bike.'

'You can't ride that thing. You're not old enough.'

'I don't mean ride it on my own. I mean with her. She says she'll take me camping in the summer.'

'I never heard of such a thing. Careering around the countryside on a motorbike. Miss Goschalk ought to know better.'

Ruth started to protest, but then Arthur chipped in.

'Don't be too hasty, Mary. I'm sure Miss Goschalk is very sensible. I don't think she goes "careering around" as you put it. I'd certainly rather Ruth went out with Miss Goschalk than racing round the fields on Jim Spencer's wreck of a machine… or something,' he added, remembering that Mary was not supposed to know what Ruth got up to in the field by the mill. 'We'll see, Ruth. Next summer's a long way off but I think you could go with Miss Goschalk if she really meant what she said.'

6

The Prentice's home had a mostly dismal air about it, even when Harold and his thirty-year-old daughter, Melanie, were entertaining a guest as welcome as Peter Salt. Peter was a fellow member of the congregation at the local Baptist church that Harold and Melanie attended. His deep-set eyes were the same warm brown as his neat hair, which had a sheen as fine as a horse-chestnut fresh from its case. He was a constant subject of conversation among the ladies of the church, who wondered that such a tall, athletic man remained single in his early thirties.

The delicate water glasses and fine porcelain on the neatly laid-out dining table had been in the family for a generation, but the exquisitely crocheted table linen was Melanie's own work. The table stood as an island of beauty in the dull fog of the room around it. Even though Harold never smoked in the dining room before meals, it was as though a tobacco haze always hung in it, imprisoned by the drab wallpaper and blackened oak furnishings. The dead acoustics of the room absorbed the words of the diners like parched earth sucking in fine rain.

Harold Prentice spoke gravely about matters of religion while Peter Salt responded with surprising enthusiasm. Melanie listened out of politeness rather than interest. Her dress was unassuming, grey and lifeless. Her superbly planned, simple meal went unremarked by the two men, but she would never have expected any comment, whether in praise or criticism.

The discussion tonight was all about the story of the

tower of Babel and its relevance to life in modern Europe. Both men had a lot to say about it but they did not seem to move towards any sort of conclusion. They interrupted their conversation only briefly from time to time, to accept from Melanie more of each dish that she pushed towards them. With the last slivers of elderberry and apple pie they seemed to be close to exhausting their chosen topic of conversation, and Melanie took the opportunity to interject.

'Shall we retire to the lounge for coffee?'

The men accepted, as she knew they would, at the prospect of sinking into the soft armchairs close to the fire for a few minutes, before proceeding with the usual highlight of these evenings together. Peter's voice was unprepossessing, perhaps even irritating, Melanie sometimes thought. She'd had ample opportunity to conclude this, as she listened to his conversations with her father. But when he opened his mouth to sing, it was as though he kept an entirely separate set of vocal cords for the purpose. His magnificent tenor would not have been out of place in a professional concert. Harold's voice, although unremarkable, was not at all bad, and Melanie was a talented pianist.

While the men helped themselves to second cups of coffee from the pot, Melanie sat at the piano and played a medley of introductions to tunes from Schumann to Cole Porter. The men were soon humming along and when she played a few bars lead-in to the inevitable duet from *The Pearl Fishers* the men burst into song. The hearts of three lonely people warmed as they were drawn close by the wonderful sounds their collaboration made.

Harold asked for something by Schubert, and Melanie's tentative few notes of *Winterreise* received Peter's immediate nod of acceptance. He sang the whole cycle in German. As the organ-grinder danced his last, faltering steps, the singer and pianist glanced at each other, looked towards Harold and saw through their own swimming sight that there were tears on his cheeks.

They averted their eyes and remained silent for a few seconds, before Melanie let forth an improvised introduction to 'Fascinating Rhythm' in a flood of notes. Her voice joined the others as they galloped through half a dozen Gershwin classics.

The warmth of feeling in the little room was so great that 'Summertime' did not seem at all out of place at the end of a December evening. The three returned to the chairs by the fire and drank cups of cocoa, before Harold fetched Peter's coat and discreetly wandered away into the kitchen. Melanie accompanied Peter to the door.

'Goodbye, Peter. I can't wait to see you again next week.'

Despite the words, her voice had a formal, almost sombre, tone. Peter gave her a slight, uneasy smile as she opened the door for him.

'Yes. Thanks for doing *Winterreise* with me.'

He hesitated, as though undecided about how to behave, before simply saying, 'Bye, Melanie,' and walking away.

Harold had started on the washing up, and with Melanie's help it was soon done.

'Good night, my dear,' Harold said to Melanie, 'and God bless.'

As he scrubbed his teeth, he thought how lucky it was that Peter Salt seemed set to become his son-in-law. He could not think of a match that would please him more. It was not just the common bond of music. Peter was a thoroughly likeable man. He was good-natured and considerate, very reliable, quite well-off and deeply involved in the life of the village Baptist church. He showed none of the unseemly lustfulness that Harold noticed in many young men. Harold felt comfortable leaving Melanie and Peter alone together, knowing that Peter would never take improper advantage of his charge.

Harold's spirit had been uplifted by the evening, and he

gave thanks for it as he knelt in his pyjamas beside his bed, but he had not long been settled before gloomier feelings returned. The last few years had been a miserable grind, since his wife had died weeks after she had been hit by an overhanging load on a lorry as it sped through the village. His thoughts went back, as they often did, to the happiness he had known when she was alive. Time and again he had asked in his prayers why it fell to him to suffer so and if there were not a way out of it. Then he would feel ashamed to be pleading for his petty needs in a world so full of sorrow, and he would turn to prayers of penitence. This evening, he once more drifted into sleep in such prayers, finding merciful escape from the dark waves that rolled over him.

He did not know what time he woke again, but it seemed like the middle of the night. His thoughts were about Lena Goschalk, the games mistress. She fascinated him in a way that confused him. She was not at all like his former wife and yet he found her intensely attractive. At this hour of the night, with his inhibitions lifted by his half-sleeping state, his mind roamed freely. He watched her as she lounged in the corner of the staff room with one foot tucked under her and her white shorts crumpled back almost indecently.

In his mind his hands stroked her ankles and then crept up towards her knees and beyond, and under his bedclothes they moved over his own body in sympathy with his thoughts. A little voice of conscience pleaded ineffectually; a compulsion born of the devil was stronger. He slipped his hand inside his pyjamas and started to work a rhythmical accompaniment to his evolving fantasy. For a few moments he felt a great wave of joy flooding over him, and then there was a terrible anti-climax as his mind returned to the reality of the wet mess in his pyjamas. He buried his face in his pillow and as he drifted back to sleep, he was deep in anguished prayer for forgiveness and the strength to exercise self-control.

7

In spring 1963, Peter Salt sat at home marking up a new setting of an Easter hymn that he had come across, adapting it to suit the small choir at the Baptist church. It was a still, pleasant, spring evening and the sash window was raised a little, allowing the scent of hyacinths planted in the garden beneath it to drift in. The sun was already low in the sky and its amber light fell across the score he was working on, giving it a warm glow. As he was getting towards the end of the job, the telephone rang. He went through to the hall to answer it, taking the score with him, and held the receiver against his ear with his shoulder while he continued to scan down the last page.

'Hello, Peter Salt speaking.'

There was a long silence. Peter was about to say 'hello' again when the voice spoke at the other end of the line.

'Can I ask you something?'

'Sorry, who is it?'

There was another pause.

Peter pencilled a note in the margin of his score. He read down a few bars and circled a pair of notes, waiting impatiently for the caller to continue.

'I really want to find some men friends, if you know what I mean… from what I've heard…'

Peter thought his encounters with male strangers were anonymous. This sounded like a trap.

'You can come along to church with me if you like. You'd meet a lot of friendly people there.'

'I don't know.'

'Come this Sunday. I'll meet you at the gate.'

'I've got to go – somebody's come in.'

The stranger rang off. From his voice, Peter guessed he was in his late twenties, which made him an attractive prospect. But it was not important whether the man was attractive or not. If he was genuine, he must be desperate, to have had the courage to ring up. Peter thought about the longing for affection that had pervaded his life before he took to the streets to find lovers. Had he treated the caller too dismissively?

Perhaps it was for the best. Getting mixed up with somebody trying to sort themselves out would be a mistake. Leading two lives was the only option for men like Peter, given the way the world was. The enforced day to day pretence made it hard enough to stay sane without taking on other people's woes.

Three or four weeks went by before the stranger called again. This time it was on a Saturday afternoon, when Peter was just finishing painting the front door. He went to the telephone with the brush still in his hand.

'Hello, it's me.'

Peter recognised the voice straight away.

'It's nice to hear from you again.'

'What are you doing?'

'Painting the front door. Do you want to come to church tomorrow?'

'Can't we meet today?'

It was unwise to agree but the stranger sounded genuine. And he had an alluring voice. It would be surprising if someone out to make trouble had waited so long before calling again. Maybe the safest place would be the village pub.

'I can meet you tonight if you like. Do you know where the Golden Lion is?'

'I don't go to pubs. Can't we meet now? I'm outside

Woolworth's.'

'Oh, you're in town.'

The busy shopping street at three in the afternoon sounded safe. If Peter drove past Woolworth's on the way to the public car park, he would be able to get a good look at the stranger before deciding whether to approach him.

'All right. I'll be about twenty minutes. How will I recognise you?'

'I've got a carrier bag from Partridge's and a blue raincoat over my arm.'

Peter stood the paintbrush in a jar of spirit for later attention and went out, leaving the front door open because of the wet paint. When he drove along the main street in town and slowed down outside Woolworth's, he saw a much younger person waiting there than he had expected, surely only fifteen or sixteen. Although he recognised him from the village, where he had seen him often, he did not really know him. *Poor kid*, Peter thought. He stopped, reached over to open the passenger door, and called the youth across, trying to work out who he was. *Got it*, he thought, *it must be Gregson's boy.*'

Tim got into the car and they set off again. His heart raced – half with fear, half with thrilled anticipation.

'It's a nice afternoon,' said Peter. 'Let's go up to the castle mound and find somewhere to sit and talk.'

They sat high on the slope of the castle mound, looking down on some cows grazing in a field across the river. The castle warden had been busy earlier in the day and there was a strong smell of newly mown grass. Peter did not need to initiate the conversation with a comforting preamble. Tim started talking the moment they were settled. He could not have been more direct.

'I fancy men so much I can hardly stop myself going for them.'

He was neither ashamed nor distressed. He found it fun to share his thoughts with someone who, he assumed, had the same compulsions. Peter had had the same urge to share his feelings, many times on many days, when he was younger. He still did, but he was rarely the first to confide in anyone. The same went for acting on his feelings. Even were that not the case, he knew how dangerous it would be to take advantage of a vulnerable teenager.

'You need to take care – especially at your age. You'll get yourself into big trouble if you try touching up a man who objects to it.'

Tim smiled as though he did not care. 'I suppose it's safer to do it with people you don't know. One of my friends says people meet in the toilets by the park.'

'There are men who will take advantage of you,' Peter said. 'You're attractive – you must realise that. Young men get raped as well as young women. And there are men roving around who'll have sex with you just so that they can turn round and blackmail you.'

He noticed a flicker of uncertainty in Tim's face. Despite his forthrightness, there was a kind of innocence about him.

'Don't look so scared. I'm only saying you need to be cautious.'

He remembered about the front door standing ajar and the paintbrush waiting for attention.

'Look at the time! I'd better drop you off in town. You can call me for a chat any time you want to, now that we've seen each other face to face.'

They returned to the car. As they got in, Peter reassured Tim again and repeated that he was welcome to telephone. Tim nodded, but Peter could see that he felt shunned by the hurried ending to their meeting.

'Can't we get a cup of coffee?' asked Tim.

Peter pointed out that it would take an age to find

somewhere to park and then walk to a coffee bar. 'I don't want to hang about. I left the front door open when I came out.'

'Why can't we go to your house then?'

Peter could guess what people would think if they were seen entering his house together. He made sure he maintained a respectable image in the village. As he saw it, it did not matter how clean-living you appeared to be – or were, come to that – if you were a single man beyond his early twenties, assumptions were made. Unexpressed most of the time, they lurked, waiting to break out if invited by the slightest rumour. But he did not want to seem harsh and unsympathetic.

Back at the house, Tim offered to clean the paint brush while Peter made the coffee. After the cleaning was done, Tim went through to Peter in the kitchen and sat on a stool by the table. He put one elbow on the table and noticed for the first time that there was paint on his sleeve.

'Oh, God. What am I going to say when I get home?'

Peter found a piece of cloth and dabbed solvent on the paint mark while they talked.

It had been a long struggle, full of doubts, before he had admitted his sexuality even to himself. Tim spoke about feeling isolated but not about shame or guilt. While still an adolescent, he seemed to have achieved greater self-acceptance, Peter thought, than he ever would. He assured Tim he was not alone and would find men of his own age who felt the way he did if he was patient, but he cautioned him to keep his true nature secret from his everyday friends if he wanted to remain part of village life.

'There you are,' said Peter. 'That won't show when it's dry.'

'So what about the toilets by the park?' Tim asked. 'I didn't believe the things written on the walls – I mean, I thought they were written by dirty-minded kids – but my friend says they're true. You go there, don't you? I've seen your car.'

Peter blushed and did not admit to the hours he spent

hunting for excitement.

'Places like that are dangerous. You could get beaten up or worse – you could get caught by the police. Have you heard about the "pretty policeman" traps? They send a young officer in tight jeans to hover about and behave provocatively. If you look him up and down and smile, that's it. You've given yourself away.'

To distract Tim from asking more probing questions, and to avoid drifting back into cataloguing threats when he should be offering reassurance, Peter asked him about his hobbies. They were soon talking about Tim's dreams of going rock-climbing and time slipped by until Peter decided he should bring the evening to an end.

'It's ten to ten,' he said. 'You ought to go home. Do you want to walk back, or shall I drop you somewhere near?'

'I can't go home now! I said I was going to stay at a friend's if I wasn't back by nine.'

'You can say you missed the bus.'

'They're all going out.' Tim put his hand into his pocket as though searching for something but failing to find it. 'I didn't bring a key. If I go home in the morning, they'll think I'm just coming back from my friend's.'

Peter knew it was not wise to let Tim stay but he seemed to need to escape from home. Perhaps there were issues he had not talked about.

'Come on. Help me make up the bed in the spare room.'

As he lay in his own bed a few minutes later, Peter thought about the boy in the room next to his who was so self-aware and so self-accepting. Peter had realised that his own interest in men set him apart from the majority by the time he was ten years old. He had longed to find someone mature and experienced who would love him for who he was. Illogical though that made it, he could not shake off the popular fallacy that youths deviated only because they were led astray by older men. But it was Tim who had initiated the contact – and with some determination.

He was drifting into sleep when he heard a gentle knock on his bedroom door, which opened slowly.

'I want to sleep in your bed,' whispered a little voice.

8

Harold Prentice had waited until 1963 before he started up his Venture Scout group, so that there were enough teenage boys with basic scouting experience ready for promotion from Arthur Hollingworth's troop. The first event was a camping weekend at Wetton Mill. When they woke up there, after the first night, the camping ground was sodden. Pools of water lay on the service track and rain was still teeming from a leaden sky. The river was a swirling brown torrent, and that gave Harold an idea.

'Come on, lads,' he yelled. 'Out of the tents. Waterproofs on. Let's get breakfast as fast as we can and start moving.'

Breakfast was not as fast as he had hoped. The rain kept running down the sides of the pans and putting out the gas, which was burning feebly anyway on account of the cold. He remembered the days when you could light a decent campfire that would cook everything and keep you warm at the same time, however much it rained. But fires were not favoured by the campsite owner, who had to think about local authority regulations and his neighbours downwind. The meal did get finished, albeit much later than Harold had intended, and he led the boys to the river.

'Today's challenge is to rig up a method for speedy, regular transit of people across the river. Who knows what a Tyrolean traverse is?'

Harold had served with the commandos during the Second World War. It was not something he talked about much, but he was one of the men who returned safely from the 'Operation Chariot' raid in St Nazaire. He had been sent on the mission immediately after a short, tough spell at a centre in Braemar, where the training had included an introduction to mountaineering.

There was no response from the boys.

'I learned about it from a famous climber called Major John Hunt. You might know his name. He led the expedition to climb Mount Everest in 1953 when you were only about seven or eight. We are going to fix a rope above the river so that personnel can hang from it and haul themselves across. The first problem is how to get a line over to the other side to start with.'

'We could go along the branch of that half-fallen tree that hangs over the water and then jump,' one of the boys pointed out.

'Indeed we could. It looks a long way to jump, but I think it is possible.'

He tied a knot in the end of a length of rope and clipped it onto his belt with a karabiner.

'Now, lads, pass out the rope while I work my way across the branch.'

The boys took hold of different bits of the pink and white rope, and Harold started along the branch, hanging from it and progressing across hand over hand. It was not far, but by the time he was halfway, Harold was thoroughly out of breath and finding that his arms, left to make their own decisions, would shortly be giving up the struggle. Worse than that, he realised that from where he was, it looked too far to swing himself from the end of the branch onto the opposite bank of the river. He started to work back towards the boys, hoping he had the strength to hang on, but he was conscious of the need to put on an impressive show and so he decided to have another try. After all, if he fell off, he would only get wet. He went as far as he could along the branch again until it sagged and creaked, swung his legs a few times to build up momentum and launched himself forwards. To his surprise he found he was on a perfect trajectory for a safe, dry landing.

He never did find out whether the boys tightened the rope deliberately, or if it was pure accident that it got caught round Harvey Beecham's ankle, as was later claimed. His flight was cut short as the rope snatched hard at his waist. It was so sudden, and he was so unprepared, that his arms and legs shot out straight in front of him and he landed on his bottom in the river. The water swept over his head and he felt his breathing paralysed by the shocking coldness of it. He bobbed to the surface, still unable to breathe, and found himself racing downstream.

On the river bank, Harvey Beecham was being dragged along on his back, the rope wrapped round his ankle, with two other boys in tow just behind, flat on their faces. Simon came on at the back, still upright, but careering across the wet grass like a water-skier making a fast turn. Harold grabbed the rope in a vain effort to stop himself, and it pulled him under the water again. He did not have the presence of mind to let go and as he bowled along the stony riverbed, with the rush of water in his ears, he gulped mouthfuls of water and began to choke.

Harvey Beecham got his leg free too late, and he, too, plunged into the water. Fortunately it was shallow close to the side, and he managed to stumble back to dry land. He joined the other three, who had come to a stop and were playing Harold on the end of the rope. Twice he surfaced but then he disappeared for a long time.

'I think we'd better let him go,' said Simon.

They let go of the rope, which whipped through their hands into the water.

Mr Prentice surfaced and floated downstream until he was beached on a shingle bank. They ran to him and helped him up into the field. He was in a bad way, but he endeavoured to get up and walk. It was not just that he was concerned about his image with the boys. What might failure signify about his advancing years and the decay of his nicotine-imbued, unexercised body? The boys helped him back to the camp where he put on dry clothes and got into his tent while they made him a warm drink.

9

The weather could not have been more different when Simon brought Tim to Wetton Mill a few weeks later. His father had bought him his own tent for his sixteenth birthday, and the boys had come away to try it out for the first time. The ground was so dry that there were patches of brown grass on the campsite, and the river was only a gentle stream of clear water. The boys sat in front of the tent at the start of the day, discussing plans, while they ate sausages and beans at the same time as bread spread with blackcurrant jam.

'We could go to the copper mines with a torch and see how far they go.'

'It won't be far. They wun't let yer in if it was.'

'Let's go the other way, then, and look at Thor's Cave.'

They packed food to take with them, which was just as well since it was almost lunch time when they set off.

The boys had been told that just down the valley, the river disappeared underground. Simon was hoping to see the river plunging over the lip of a bottomless chasm, and so the boys found a way down to the site by the side of a bridge. When they got there, they were disappointed. The water just soaked away through the stones, leaving the riverbed beyond dry and half overgrown with wild rhubarb. Simon poked around with sticks, and Tim jumped up and down on the stones but nothing happened. So the boys carried on with the trek. They followed the bare riverbed for quite a long way in the hope of finding where the water reappeared but, realising they were going to run out of time to visit Thor's Cave, they decided to leave the hunt for the resurgence for another day.

When they got to the top of the steep path to the cave, they found a young man and woman preparing to climb on the limestone face beside the entrance.

'Let's look inside and then watch them climb while we eat,' said Simon, already noticing how good-looking the man was.

They dumped their packs and scrambled into the cave. The exploration did not take long. There was one exciting dark bit, but it did not go anywhere. They were soon outside again, sitting in the sunshine in a good position to watch the climbers. By the time the boys had got their peanut butter and banana sandwiches out, the man had already started to climb and the woman was belaying him from below. He was about twenty feet off the ground and busy pulling bits of metalwork from a tape hung round his neck, to find one that fitted into a crack above him. He chose one, slipped it into the crack and pulled hard at it. Then he attached a length of tape to it and clipped his rope onto the end with a karabiner.

'Take in on green,' he called, and the woman pulled the rope tight.

All this time he had been leaning back from the cliff face with one toe on a tiny bump on the rock, his other foot against a vertical flake level with his waist, and hanging from a ledge no wider than the edge of a box of matches with one hand. The boys looked on in wonder at his skill and strength. Preoccupied with admiring his physical beauty, they said nothing to each other. Muscles rippled in his powerful arms and across his bronzed back, and his dark blue tights outlined the details of his legs and lower torso.

He rocked even further back for a moment and then jumped for another tiny hold with his free hand. Pulling his weight up on the one arm, he brought his feet to a more secure ledge. He let his breath whistle through his teeth, and flashed a smile down to his girlfriend. Tim and Simon gasped, too, at the relief of the tense moment. After that the man seemed to edge his way almost effortlessly to the top of the steep face, pausing in a couple of places to put more bits of metalwork into cracks and clip his rope into them. He disappeared for a while, shouting instructions, and then he reappeared, seated himself with his legs dangling over the cliff edge and pulled in the ropes.

'That's me on green,' shouted the woman. 'That's me on purple.'

'Climb when you're ready.'

'Climbing.'

She started to climb, and Tim and Simon watched the man, sun-gilded against the blue sky, taking in the ropes through a device attached to his harness. The woman was a good climber and she progressed with ease to the crux, where the boys had started watching the man in action. Their attention was drawn from him to her as she took out the gear he had left hanging from the crack and prepared for the fearsome leap to attain the hold above. For her it was a bigger challenge, since her reach was inches less than his, but she sprang effortlessly. The boys mouthed their admiration as they watched her complete the climb.

Once she was safe, the man looked down at the boys.

'Don't go away. We'll be down in a minute.'

The boys packed away their empty lunch boxes and pop bottles, and waited. The man hooked the mid-point of a rope into a karabiner hanging just over the edge of the crag, threw down both ends, and abseiled to the ground, bouncing from foot to foot against the white rock.

'Hello, I'm Chris. Do you want a go?'

'Yeah!'

Chris glanced towards his girlfriend who had just come round the corner after walking down from the climb on a path to one side of the crag.

'Bring us the spare harness, Nic.'

He turned back to the boys.

'That's Nicola. Who are you?'

'Simon.'

'Tim.'

'Okay. Who's going first? Simon?'

'No, go on. You go, Tim.'

Chris helped Tim to put on the spare harness and attached it to the end of the rope.

'You're not trying for anything quite so hard yet. Nic'll show you.'

Nicola strolled across to the foot of the cliff and climbed up a wide crack without even the rope to protect her. It looked easy.

'Okay, your turn, Tim. What do you do first?'

'Left hand up there?'

'What about the pile of rope in front of you? Say it: "take in".'

'Take in,' Tim said, self-consciously.

The rope came tight but Chris kept pulling so hard that Tim was nearly lifted off his feet.

'Forgotten anything?'

'Oh,' replied Tim. 'That's me.'

'Climb when you're ready.'

Tim launched himself onto the rock. After he had gone about ten feet up, he seemed to get stuck. Nobody said anything for a while, until he called down, 'Now what?'

'Not as easy as it looks, is it? Swap feet.'

'I dursn't do that!'

'Yes, you dare. Just hop.'

'I'm coming down.'

'You're going up.'

Tim made an ineffectual half jump, lost his footing and fell off. The rope held him, but he grabbed it with both hands all the same.

'I told you, you wouldn't fall. Let go of the rope, lean back and stand against the rock.'

Tim obeyed and let his arms dangle by his side. Reassured by how safe that made him feel, he pulled himself back onto the rock, making sure he had his feet the right way round this time, reached for another hold and continued the climb. The rest of it was easy and he bounded to the top. Nicola went up, untied him and threw the rope-end down again.

When Tim had walked back down to Chris and Simon, Chris took the harness from him and helped Simon to put it on. Being so close, Simon could not help staring at the bulge in Chris's tights framed by the straps of his harness, even though he tried not to do. He wanted to reach out and touch it, and he was aware that the bulge in his own jeans was growing larger. He was relieved that Chris did not seem to notice as he fiddled around tying on the rope.

'That's it,' said Chris.

He tugged the rope to demonstrate that it was secure, and Simon felt the straps of the harness tighten around his crotch.

He stepped over to the foot of the climb and remembered to call, 'Take in.'

'That's me,' he called, feeling the pull of the rope again.

'Climb when you're ready.'

'Climbing.'

The rock was warm to Simon's fingers as he gripped the secure holds, and he immediately felt at one with it. All other thoughts floated away. He was a happy primate, reunited with his territory. He had the advantage of having watched Tim, and when he came to the tricky problem of swapping feet, he did it easily, if not with particular elegance. Style was a consideration which would come to his attention when he had a good deal more experience.

Then in his anxiety to do well, he scrambled too quickly and missed a foothold. His arms saved him, and he pulled himself back on.

'Take it easy,' shouted Nic, looking down from above. 'It's not a race.'

After Simon had completed the climb, the boys made it clear they were eager to do more, but Chris and Nic could not stay. They did not even offer their telephone number – if they had one – or address, and Tim and Simon did not ask. They stood in the cave mouth and watched the couple go hand in hand down the path into the trees, and then descended into the valley themselves and walked back to the campsite.

Simon had long believed himself to be lacking in masculinity, despite being tougher and more audacious than many of his pals. He had joined the Venture Scouts to prove himself, but they were a tame disappointment.

Perceiving himself to be faint-hearted, he reasoned that if he was brave enough to do something, it could not be a truly brave thing to do. When he accepted the invitation to climb from Chris, he thought he was at last taking on the supreme test of courage, but climbing turned out not to be frightening – exciting, but not frightening. Climbing was about something more sublime than the crude outfacing of danger.

During the evening the boys talked of nothing but Nic and Chris, and climbing – the feel of the rock, the taste and smell of it on their fingers. They wanted to spend the rest of their lives on cliff faces in the sunshine, modelling themselves into copies of Nic and Chris, able to re-enact the beauty of their flowing movements. They were still talking about it after they fastened up the tent for the night and got into their sleeping bags. They lay close to each other and wondered where the two climbers were, and what they were doing.

'I bet they're lying side by side with their arms round each other,' said Tim.

'She's probably stroking his tights,' Simon said.

'You noticed his tights, then.'

'A bit stupid if you ask me,' Simon said.

'They showed his body off.'

'S'pose so. Well, yeah… What does he do if he gets a hard on? Everybody'd be able to see.'

'Dunno.'

Tim rolled closer to Simon. Simon's hand, lying beside his body, could feel the hard lump inside Tim's sleeping bag pressed against it. He moved his fingers slightly, not wanting to make it too obvious. Tim did not move away. Simon was starting to find the restriction of his own underpants uncomfortable. He slipped his free hand down and lifted the waistband.

'What yer doing?' Tim asked.

'Nothing.'

'Bet you wish you could be Chris in bed with Nic.'

'If I was on my own, I'd probably pretend,' he replied. 'Do you imagine things like that? You know – when you do it.'

'I can't hardly stop myself when I'm at home,' said Tim. 'We've gone without for three days now. I haven't ever gone that long – not since I was a kid, I mean.'

'I bet you I can hold it longer than you can. I bet you can't go until the end of the week.'

'Bet I can.'

There was a long pause, during which Tim turned away and they both lay on their backs, wondering how they would keep the bet through the night, let alone till the end of the week. Each had more or less decided to wait for the other to fall asleep, and then to try for secret relief, when Tim ventured an idea.

'I can't hold it all week. If I didn't do it for myself, would that count?'

Simon did not dare to respond. Tim might not have meant what he seemed to mean. He was longing to reach out and touch Tim, but the fear of giving himself away and receiving scorn instead of affection held him back. He turned to look at Tim. In the faint light of the moon, shining through the fabric of the tent, he could see him lying back with his hands under his head and his eyes half-closed. His sleeping bag was pulled tight over his body.

Simon sat up, shrugging his own sleeping bag off his naked shoulders and pushing it down to his waist. Still Tim did not move. Simon put his hand on Tim's shoulder and squeezed it. He allowed his hand to wander slowly over Tim's sleeping bag. In a few minutes he was gently stroking the exciting bulge while Tim arched his back to press himself against Simon's hand.

'Go on,' Tim said, suddenly and loudly. 'Go on.'

'Quiet over there! Don't you know what time it is?'

The voice came from another tent. The boys froze for a moment.

Without speaking, Simon slid open the zip of Tim's sleeping bag, caressed Tim's chest and stomach, and then coaxed him to a climax.

'That was nice,' whispered Tim. 'Your turn.'

'It's too late,' Simon replied.

Tim felt inside Simon's sleeping bag, and spread the slippery fluid over Simon's stomach with his fingertips.

'I'll do it for you tomorrow.'

The boys lay down and fell asleep in each other's arms, as they were to do many times after that night.

10

Lena Goschalk sat in an armchair in the school staff room, sorting through a stack of end-of-term report forms. Behind her the rain lashed against the window and rivulets of condensation formed pools on the window ledge. The door opened and she watched Harold Prentice come in with water dripping from his hair. Being wet made it seem limp and much sparser than it was. Scattered grey hairs like embellishing threads were woven into the dark brown, almost black, neatly groomed profusion that he had kept into his middle age. Combined with the near absence of thinning, even at the temples, the subtle mixing of shades made him look distinguished. When he sat in his preferred chair in the corner of the staff room to relax, doing nothing in particular and unaware of being observed, there was a gentle sadness in his eyes that aroused Lena's sympathy. Despite their age difference, she found Harold curiously attractive. There must have been twenty years between them.

She realised he had noticed her attention and chuckled. 'Thank God it was the girls' turn for the gym,' she said.

'What? Oh, my hair. I haven't dried it properly – I've just come out of the shower. You're right all the same – we got soaked. There must be two inches of water on the pitch. What can you do with a bunch of first years? If you keep them in, they start playing up. It strikes me they like getting wet as long as there's plenty of mud about. When it comes to getting wet in the showers they hate it.'

Harold walked over to his jacket, hanging on a hook near the door – the only tailored one of good-quality tweed, showing comforting signs of age and wear, among an assortment of modern, factory-made items. He took out a little packet.

'Fancy a mint?'

'Thanks. When did you take to eating peppermints?'

'I'm trying to give up smoking.'

'Well done you!'

A pile of papers slid off the arm of Lena Goschalk's chair, and she grabbed for them as they fell. She yelped and sucked her finger.

'Oh, damn. You wouldn't think paper could be so sharp. I'm supposed to be playing tonight.'

Harold looked puzzled for a moment and then said, 'Ah, clarinet. Sorry, I didn't follow you at first. I thought you were talking about playing hockey.'

Lena took a suck of her peppermint.

'I'm still going back to rehearsals every week after all this time. I never switched orchestras when I moved. I'm not sure whether to keep it up. I'd prefer something more convivial. In an orchestra you feel lost in a crowd.'

'You know I sing and so does Melanie and she plays the piano?'

Lena nodded. Harold often mentioned musical evenings with his daughter, Melanie, but only in passing.

He went on. 'We've got a tenor friend who's marvellous – Peter Salt. He lives in Church Wensley. I'm not sure if you'll know him, not living in the village yourself, but he comes to the school some evenings.'

'Is he one of the parents?'

'No. Apart from him being in the village, I know him because he's in the Baptist choir. He comes here to the Gilbert and Sullivan Society rehearsals. He's one of their lead singers. Did you go to see *Iolanthe* last year?'

'Oh! Is he the one I've heard people talking about? The

good-looking one with rich brown hair and an irresistible smile? He comes up more times than the weather in conversations between the women queuing in the Co-op across the road. I saw him in a performance but I don't know him to speak to.'

'He visits us on Monday evenings. You could do 'The Shepherd on the Rock' if you brought your clarinet.'

It was almost time for Harold to give his next lesson. He reached for his teaching gown, which was dusty with chalk and frayed at the sleeves where they had many times been caught in classroom doors.

'What about next Monday?'

'If you're sure it's all right.'

'Have dinner with us.'

So it was that Lena became a fourth regular member of the group that met at the Prentices' home, and got to know Harold and Melanie, and Peter Salt, much better.

11

Ruth eventually got her motorcycle trip to the Lake District with Lena Goschalk. They were up early on the first morning and busy preparing breakfast. Lena fried eggs on a cantankerous Primus stove, once she had got it to settle down and burn properly instead of issuing a column of fire. Ruth worked at scraping off slivers of butter, hardened by the coolness of the night, and laying them, rather than spreading them, on slices of bread. The grass was wet with dew, and they crouched to do their tasks as it was too wet to sit down. When the food was ready, they perched insecurely, side by side against the motorbike saddle to eat.

Ruth asked, 'Can I call you "Lena"?'

'Of course you can. Out of school. But carry on calling me "Miss Goschalk" in class.'

'Everybody knows we're special friends.'

'Just because we're special friends doesn't mean we can bend the rules at school. Anyway, forget about school. We're on holiday.'

Ruth was pleased they had taken a step closer, although being able to address Lena more familiarly was of limited use once they were on the road.

It would have been harder to get much nearer together – riding pillion, Ruth felt her knees locked against Lena's leather-clad legs, her body pressed against Lena's back, and her chin on Lena's right shoulder so that she could watch the road ahead. With the rush of the wind, conversation was more or less impossible.

They stopped at a gate and Ruth got off the bike to open

it. As she was fastening the latch again, she caught the smell of the moorland on the breeze and it drew her attention to the scene over the bars of the gate. On one side of the road a dark-grey stone wall topped a bank strewn with the russet remains of dead bracken still lying among the small, fresh shoots that were starting to push through. On the other side, beyond a stream, a pale-green field sloped up to red and brown hillsides and outcrops of black rock. There were sheep dotted about everywhere and tiny white clouds drifted across a blue sky. Ruth wanted to cut out the picture before her, strap it to the motorbike and take it home.

She got back onto the pillion seat. They sped off over a bridge and along a winding road open to the moors on both sides. They rounded a sharp bend and Lena accelerated up a slope so steep and rough that Ruth was in danger of falling off the back of the motorbike. She put both hands onto Lena's shoulders and clung on, enjoying the excitement. A car appeared suddenly over the brow of the hill. There was barely room even for a car and a motorcycle to pass on the narrow road. Lena reduced their speed for a moment and then accelerated into a narrowing gap between the car and a rocky buttress. The back wheel of the motorbike skipped sideways off the rough edge of the roadway and back, sending stones skittering down the hill, and they were through.

Over the top of the pass, they rolled down a steep gradient with only the softest purr from the engine as it braked their descent. Ahead, below them, the road snaked along the curved base of a glaciated valley, with not another vehicle on it.

When they were down into the valley, Lena brought the motorbike to a stop. She turned to speak to Ruth.

'Enjoying it?'

Ruth nodded.

'We can go on the Ravenglass and Eskdale Railway if you

like. It's not far and we might not get another day as good as this for it.'

Ruth had neither inherited nor acquired her father's enthusiasm for trains, and he had taken her on this one more than once, but she did not like to disappoint Lena and so she agreed.

It was not only the road over the pass that was quiet that morning. There was no one else at the station, and when they boarded a train, they found themselves sitting in complete privacy, well away from the few other passengers. The engine driver tooted the whistle and the train trundled off.

Just outside the station it made a brief stop. Ruth reached out and pulled a fresh young bud of leaves from a hawthorn bush beside the track. As the train set off again, she nibbled at the hawthorn bud and started a conversation with Lena Goschalk.

'Did you mean it, about us being special friends?'

'I wouldn't have said it if I didn't.'

The hawthorn bud did not really taste like bread and cheese, even if that was what people called it.

'So we can talk about anything.'

'It might depend what it is.'

'Oh.'

The click of the wheels on the track counted out the passing minutes while Ruth considered what to say. There was something unreal about riding in an open-air train and being able to hear the birds in the trees as they passed by.

The engine breathed a few more deep breaths; the wheels clicked on a few more minutes.

'I've got this friend… She thinks she might have fallen in love with somebody, only she doesn't know if she should say anything in case they don't feel the same about her.'

'It's like that, falling in love,' Lena said.

'She told me, she's tried dropping hints but they don't seem to get anywhere.'

'To tell you the truth,' said Lena, 'I'm not the best person to advise you. I've got much the same problem, believe it or not.'

The remark intrigued Ruth, but before she could frame a question, Lena had moved on.

'She needs to get to know him better. Can't she ask him to go to a party or something – or find out from his friends what he's interested in, and get interested in the same thing?'

'Oh, it isn't a him – it's a her,' said Ruth. 'That's the problem. It would be easy if it was a boy. But it isn't – it's a woman. It isn't even another girl – it's a teacher.' She paused for a moment. 'That's why she daren't say anything. It's not something she can go telling people, is it?'

'I don't see why women shouldn't fall in love with each other. But if you want to know if I'm a lesbian – no, I'm not.'

'Oh, God, I'm sorry,' said Ruth.

'Schoolgirls often think they have fallen in love with their teachers, but they go off them when they get to know them better. I'll be your friend, but I can't love you back that way. You need to find a girlfriend more your own age. It's not what I'm supposed to say. I hate to think what the headmaster would say if he heard me, but unofficially it's what I think you ought to do.'

Ruth stared at Lena in astonishment. 'It isn't you! I'm not in love with you! It's Melanie Prentice.'

She was not sure whether to interpret Lena's expression as one of relief or offence. She turned to watch the passing scenery. Now that they were among the trees in the valley, it was gloomy compared with the sunny fell they had ridden down from.

'She teaches at the Sunday School. I just want to be with her all the time. I'm sure she wouldn't approve if she found out.'

'Come on,' Lena said. 'It's not like you to let things get you down. At least you've got me to talk to.'

Ruth smiled. 'Yes.'

There was a short pause, and then Ruth, still looking out into the trees, spoke again. 'Who is that you fancy?'

'I'll tell you another time.'

12

'Now then, young man, I think we'd better have a word or two. How long would you say you've been in there?'

Tim stood in the doorway of the public lavatories, staring into the face of a policeman.

'Dunno. Five minutes?'

'Fifteen. Fifteen minutes. What were you in there for?'

'Cos I wanted a pee.'

'And it took fifteen minutes.'

'S'pose so.'

'Pee a lot, do you?'

Tim looked back blankly.

'Four times this afternoon,' continued the policeman. 'Come on.'

Tim had never really believed this could happen. He had read the condemnatory reports in the local paper when someone came up before the bench. Peter had warned him that the police kept a close watch on the toilets and never missed an opportunity to apprehend anyone who threatened to behave improperly. But things like that happened to other people. It did not occur to him to do anything other than to follow the policeman to the car parked among the shrubs across the road, and ride with him to the police station.

The policeman took down Tim's name and address.

'Do you want a cup of tea?'

'I don't think I'd better.'

'No, perhaps not, under the circumstances. So, let's get this straight – you went into the toilets for a pee and it took you fifteen minutes.'

'Yes.'

'And you went to some others twenty minutes before that, different ones an hour before that, and different ones again just after lunch time.' 'Yes.'

'...for a pee – every time.'

Tim ran his finger round and round a circular mark left on the desk by a hot mug and said nothing.

'And where did you go in between these visits? Let's start with when you left home this morning.'

'I didn't. I stayed at home until after lunch. I came into town on my bike to go shopping and on the way I stopped at the toilets.'

'What did you buy when you got into town?'

'Some records. They're with my bike.'

Tim had been so disoriented by his arrest that he had forgotten his bicycle, unlocked, leaning against the side wall of the lavatories with his records in a carrier bag tucked beside the back wheel.

'Then I was going to go home,' he continued.

'And you called at the toilets again on your way.'

'Yes.'

The policeman grunted and shifted in his chair.

'You didn't go home. You went back into town.'

'I left my records in the café.'

The policeman tutted impatiently, put his hands flat on the desk and leaned towards Tim.

'You already had the records with you when you went back into town. I watched you put the bag on your handlebars. Haven't you been told it's dangerous, hanging things on your handlebars?'

He waited for a response. Getting none, he went on. 'You didn't go to the toilets at the bus station for another pee by any chance, did you?'

'One record it was. I took one out to look at it and then I

left it behind.'

'What record?'

'I forget.'

'You took it out to look at it, but you forget what it was.'

'Yes – no. It was Eartha Kitt.'

'Eartha Kitt!'

'Yes.'

'So, after you'd retrieved it, you went back to the toilets by the park for a pee that took fifteen minutes.'

'Yes.'

'Where did you go for this pee?'

Tim did not understand.

'In a cubicle?' the policeman asked.

'In one of the stalls.'

'You didn't go into the cubicles?'

'Only sort of.'

'What do you mean, sort of?'

'I went for a pee, but then I thought I wanted to do something else. I went into a cubicle but I changed my mind.'

'And it took you fifteen minutes altogether.'

'I had a pee, but I couldn't decide if I wanted to do something else.'

'Did you speak to the man who came in just after you?'

'Somebody went into a cubicle.'

'Which one?'

'I don't know. The middle one, probably.'

'And which one did you use?'

'I didn't. I only went in and came out. The one at the end.'

'Was that while the other man was in the middle one?'

Tim remained silent and tried to look as though he was at a loss to remember.

'There's something special about that cubicle.'

'How do you mean?'

'There's a hole in the partition.'

'Oh, that. Yes.'

'Big enough to put your hand through into the middle cubicle. Let's stop beating about the bush, sonny boy. You were in there for homosexual purposes. We've watched you going in and out often enough. You ought to be ashamed of yourself. Messing about with men in toilets.'

He started to hand photographs to Tim of men crossing the road outside the toilets.

'I wonder which of these got you into the habit.'

Tim recognised none of them until they came to the last picture. It was of Peter Salt getting into his car. Tim knew that a flicker of recognition had crossed his face. The policeman left the photograph on the desk and put the others away. The sliding of the drawer and the thump as it closed sounded like the fall of the guillotine.

'I'd better let your father know where you are.'

He reached for the telephone but did not lift the receiver.

'What were you doing on Wednesday night?'

Tim constructed a hurried answer: 'I went to choir practice.'

The policeman turned his partially clenched free hand palm upwards, and pointed sideways to the photograph with his thumb.

'With him.'

'I went with a friend. We've both got solos to sing.'

The policemen nodded at the photograph. 'In his house.'

'The heating wasn't on in the church.'

'When did this practice finish?'

'I don't know exactly. Not all that late.'

'So how did you come to be getting out of Peter Salt's car outside the school gates on Thursday morning?'

'It wasn't me.'

'Don't play games with me,' the policeman replied sternly. 'I sat and watched you.'

After a long silence he picked up the telephone and started to dial. 'Let's see where your father thinks you were on Wednesday night.'

'Don't call him. I did stay. Just that night.'

The policeman put the telephone down again.

'Fancy good-looking older men? Or did he talk you into it?'

'It's not what you think. He isn't like that. He's kind.'

'Oh!'

'My parents were out. I forgot my key, so he said I could sleep in the spare room.'

'Like on all the other nights you've stayed there.'

Tim had been depending on his assumption that he had only been seen once with Peter. He looked pleadingly at the policeman.

'I didn't want to tell you because I knew you'd think all the wrong things.'

The pleading had its effect.

'Let's leave it at that. I can see you've been led astray. Don't let me catch you around those toilets again. Mend your ways while you're still young enough to grow up normal. You should have more sense than to get mixed up with perverts.'

Tim followed the policeman out of the building. He was hardly aware of getting into the car and travelling back to collect his bicycle. His mind was busy with working out how he'd been caught out, and how to avoid it in future.

13

Peter Salt was having a shower before breakfast when the knock came on his door. He wrapped a towel round himself and ran dripping wet down the stairs, cursing the inconvenience of getting such an early call from what he assumed would be the postman with a special delivery. The policeman who stood at the door asked him to get dressed and come to the police station.

Peter was so law-abiding in all but one respect that it was obvious to him the police knew something about his illicit sex life. He had heard stories from men he encountered about what had happened to some of the people they knew. One man had been sent down for ten years. A teenage boy had been taken away from his parents and put into care. He had hanged himself. A gentle young man, like Tim. Even being bound over and ending up in the papers was enough to break a lonely, older man, disgraced for seeking affection.

As he rode in the back of the police car, Peter thought about how he would defend himself. It was his belief that a lot of the men whose names appeared in the court proceedings columns of the local paper caved in too easily under questioning. They were so troubled by moral guilt that they mistook it for predetermined criminal guilt, and confessed without a fight. Peter was a victim of moral guilt, too – many were the hours he had bowed beneath the strictures of his conscience – but he understood the difference. If the police wanted to prosecute him, he was going to make it hard for them to prove their case.

On arrival at the police station, the constable closed the

door and signalled Peter to a chair. He sat down himself, picked up a pen, filled something in on a form, and then commented, 'You know why you are here, of course.'

He held out the photograph of Peter getting into his car opposite the park toilets that he had shown to Tim. 'We've been watching people going in and out for the last four weeks. We know all the regulars.'

'I'm sorry – when did it become an offence to use a public toilet?'

The policeman opened a new packet of cigarettes, took one out and lit it. He dealt out the other photographs to Peter, one by one, that he had previously shown to Tim. Peter denied ever having seen any of the men before. The policeman took the photographs back, selected one like a conjurer pulling a card from the pack, and put it in front of Peter. He opened the drawer of his desk, took out another picture and laid it down beside the first. Both images showed the same person, but in the second, he was opening the passenger door of Peter's car. The policeman sat back and waited for Peter to speak.

Peter said nothing.

'How well do you know Tim Gregson?'

Had they only seen Tim getting into his car in town the first time he brought him home, and built a case on it, or did they know more than that?

'He's in the choir I run. His family aren't church-goers. I think he just attends because he likes singing. He never misses choir practice.'

'So he's been telling us.'

Peter started and the policeman noticed.

'We pulled him in yesterday. He was very helpful – positively talkative. I've heard all the old jokes, but I didn't think the duties of choirboys extended to staying overnight with the choirmaster.'

Peter took a chance, hoping that he did not say anything at odds with what Tim might have said. He waved his hand dismissively. 'Oh – is that all? I put him up while his parents were away one night.'

The policeman's irritation with Peter's evasiveness was evident from the monotone firmness of his speech. 'He's spent eight nights with you in the last month. On at least half of those occasions, the curtains of only one bedroom were drawn, and that was the only room where the light went on. Do you know what the penalty is for interfering with a teenage boy? I can get you sent down for ten years at the very least.'

Peter rubbed the side of his face with one hand.

'He'll be taken into care, of course,' the policeman continued. 'Pity – he seems a bright lad. What was he planning – university? It makes me sick to see a young life ruined by an interfering pervert.'

'Can't you leave him out of it? He's hardly more than a child.'

'Exactly.'

The policeman looked at his watch.

'It's twenty past eight. If we can settle this now, you can be away and at work on time. We know why you hang around the toilets, and why you picked this man up.' He held up the photograph of the man getting into Peter's car. 'We do know who it is, even if he does come all the way from Liverpool. Plead guilty to a simple charge of importuning and I'll drop Tim Gregson from my investigations. It's up to you. A small fine for a first offence and a promise to behave yourself in future – or a spell inside for you and a care order for Gregson.'

14

'"If thy right eye offend thee, pluck it out."

'Brothers and sisters in Christ, this week a part of the living flesh of this church and community has been torn out to leave a painful wound.

'For the first time I can remember, since it was occupied fourteen years ago by a fine young man newly graduated from the Sunday School, the end seat among the tenors of the choir is empty. The man who sat there had been an inspiration to us all – a pillar of the church on whom we leaned. Now he has fled the village in disgrace – found wanting in the eyes of the Lord and banished afar.

'How could we, a loving family, have stayed so long oblivious to the evil in our midst? How far might this cancerous iniquity have spread its tentacles among us? What other evils lurk unsuspected behind the gentle faces that I see now gravely turned towards me?'

As Harold Prentice delivered his sermon, his mind still reeled from the implications of the sordid little item in the evening paper earlier that week. To think that he had promoted friendship between his daughter and Peter Salt – that Melanie could have found herself married to one who practised the unspeakable.

'We live in a time of slackening morality. Perhaps you think that this is not all for the bad? I hear the protestations of my liberal friends even now as they argue against a return to the old hypocrisies that masqueraded as morality.

'Do not be mistaken, dear friends. It is not a return to hypocrisy that I urge. Hypocritical allegiance to principles never was and never will be an honourable thing. Our mission must be the reassertion of a true morality kept in deed, not in word – out of conviction, not just to go with the crowd.

'How easy it is to move with the sway. How especially easy and alluring to move with the sway towards laxity and degeneracy. We must strive to rid society of the curses that beset it in the best, the simplest, the only way that we have learned from our Lord: through self-discipline; adherence to the fundamental codes of morality which we all know and understand in our hearts.

'Do not point the accusing finger. Are any of us worthy to cast even the second stone? All through the scriptures we are reminded that there are no degrees of sin before the Lord. What secret vices do we each harbour? What sins do we practise unseen? Look not at one another, but at yourselves. There – there, is the root of the problem. Deep inside each of us, hidden from our brothers and sisters, hideous wickedness gnaws away. The Lord comes as a thief in the night. All that was covert is unmasked – our sins, our devotion to self-gratification, our most shameful secrets.

'Lucifer is ever at work and we must be vigilant. How was it that our brother in the face of so gross a temptation acquiesced? Was he a man run through with depravity? The man who led our choir, who led our prayers? Surely not. Yet he was tested and found wanting. He had not the faith and strength to look temptation in the face and declare, "Get thee behind me, Satan!"

'Alas he was prey to an evil so fell that I will not name it in this house of God. His sins are uncovered and he has rightly fled in shame. Is this indeed the house of God, or the Temple of Baal? Do pure hearts come here to praise the Lord, or do they beat with secret lusts and cravings barely checked?

'Feel no sorrow for the banishment of Satan and his ways.

Feel anguish for the fall of a beloved brother. Pray for his enlightenment and liberation. Pray for his return, repentant, to the fold. And if the prodigal son returns contrite, make it your duty to keep him on the true path – watch over him lest he should stray again.'

Upset though he was over the calamity that had befallen his daughter, something else was worrying Harold. It was the disquieting nature of his fascination with Lena Goschalk. It had been a while since he had first noticed something erotic about her mode of dress as she arrived at school. Yesterday he had brushed against a man in motorcycling gear in the supermarket and he had felt a thrill run all through his body at the touch of leather. It was not the touch of another man – Harold had no fears on that score – it was the leather and its association with Lena Goschalk. Harold's perception of decency classed an obsession with leather as a perversion, whether it was associated with a man or a woman. There were books depicting improper activities with women in leather that circulated among men who had fallen from grace, or so he had heard.

With the exposure of Peter Salt's other life, an even more dreadful possibility had come into Harold's mind. Was not a particular kind of woman supposed to dress in leather? He could not use the word even in his thoughts, but he could not ignore the signs: a sportswoman motorcyclist with a love of leather, who delighted in taking teenage girls away with her on camping trips. Should he have a word with the Hollingworths? Was Ruth safe?

There had been a time when he had believed he lived in a comfortable circle of God-fearing friends. He had dared to hope that he might find a second wife in Miss Goschalk. Now he found himself prey to erotic fantasies that demeaned his erstwhile pure intentions, and he saw his friends swept into the worst excesses that Satan had devised. He looked round anxiously at the faces of the congregation.

'Let us join together in prayer for our deliverance and the deliverance of all those we love.'

15

Church Wensley Village Fête was on the second Saturday in August. Records were not likely to be broken in the produce competition tent: it had been a long, hard winter and a disappointing spring. It rained in the morning, leaving the meadow wet and muddy. The sky had started to clear by midday and things seemed set to stay fair by the time of the official opening at 2 pm, though still remaining unseasonably chilly.

Harold and Lena arrived rather late in the afternoon. He had invited her to come to the fête with him when she had mentioned it a few weeks earlier.

Having always lived in one town and now another, she said she looked upon fêtes as quaint, rural events. It would be fun to visit the one in Church Wensley. Harold's own experiences at the village fête over the years had been mixed. His wife had been on the organising committee and managed the food tent and he had gone along in support. He had shown little interest in the goings on and not taken part in games or competitions. After she died, he continued to attend but still as an observer rather than a participant.

Lena came on the bus and he met her at the stop. They slithered through the mud in the narrow gateway to the field and looked around. Mrs Hollingworth, her headscarf tied firmly under her chin but still flapping gently in the cool wind, was in charge of the bring-and-buy stall. Lena noticed an old souvenir milk jug with a picture of Blackpool Tower on its side.

'Oh look. That's like the one you have.'

'It *is* the one we had. Melanie's been clearing out. There are a few other things you might recognise if you take a look.'

'What a shame. It's not very elegant but there's something intriguing about it.'

'Why don't you buy it? It's all in a good cause.'

'It's not *that* intriguing. I'm just surprised to see it there. Come on. Let's see if we can dig something thrilling out of the bran tub. It's only a shilling and, as you said, it's all in a good cause.'

Lena paid her shilling and thrust her hand into the bran tub.

'Ooh, there's something long and thin.'

She pulled out the neatly wrapped package and peeled the paper off it. It was a cigarette holder.

'Not much use to me – nor to you – now. This way…'

She led Harold back to the bring-and-buy stall and donated the cigarette holder to it.

The public address system crackled. 'Ladies and gentlemen. Just a reminder that competition entries will remain on show for the rest of the afternoon. I'll announce the results of the raffle and bowling for the pig at about 5 pm. So if you haven't had a go, do it soon before it is too late.'

Lena pointed to a sign at the far end of the field.

'Bowling for a pig! We've got to try that while there's time.'

'Lena,' said Harold, 'what would either of us do with a pig?'

'It doesn't matter. We won't win.'

She took hold of Harold's hand, and he reluctantly let himself be pulled across the field.

Half a crown bought one go, with three balls. Lena went first and, in order of attempts, missed the skittles entirely, knocked one down and then another two. She laughed. 'I told you we wouldn't win! Your go.'

Harold's first ball took out five skittles. His second ball

knocked down three more, but the last one was still standing after he had bowled his third ball.

Lena gave Harold an astonished look. He beamed and chuckled.

'Once I saw the first five go down I couldn't resist the challenge… It was a bit unwise. I ought to have put more effort into missing. I've always been good at ball games. I'll just have to hope somebody else outperforms me!'

Lena laughed and gave Harold a gentle punch on the arm. 'I'll buy you the pig sty. Let's get a cup of tea.'

The tea tent, a white marquee, was near their end of the field. They went inside. It had the overpowering, wet-grass smell that only seems to be encountered in tea tents at fêtes and pervades the flavours of everything in them. Harold had not smelt it since the year his wife died. He looked seriously at Lena for a moment, and then put on a polite smile and asked, 'Piece of cake as well?'

'Just tea for me, thanks.'

They drank their strong but over milky tea with a cut grass flavour and went outside again.

Not far from the tea tent was the 'dunk the vicar' stand. The vicar sat beneath a bucket of water. Customers threw tennis balls at a flat, wooden lever and, if they were strong and accurate enough, a mechanism tipped the bucket. The vicar had taken the precaution of putting on a waterproof jacket but he was pretty well soaked through nevertheless. 'You can't fail on this one,' Lena said.

'I couldn't do it. Not to the poor vicar.' Harold was laughing. 'It'll have to be you.'

'Just watch me!'

Lena grabbed a couple of tennis balls and hurled them in quick succession, without waiting to pay. The bucket emptied itself and the vicar shrank deeper into his jacket to minimise the effect of the deluge. Harold stepped forward and put a generous donation into the collection pot.

'We haven't looked at the competition entries yet,' said Lena. 'Let's do it now.'

In another marquee they found a row of jars of jam, each with a saucer and spoon beside it – white plates bearing three, almost-identical carrots, a further set featuring three onions and yet more with runner beans as long as the draft excluders people put under doors. Ten Victoria sponges each had a wedge neatly taken out. There were paintings by local children on the theme of 'my favourite animal'. The winning one was a magnificent lion with a blue face and a vivid red mane.

'I don't think I'd get anywhere with jam-making,' said Lena. 'And as for my cakes, the less said the better… Judging by that lion, I would not stand a chance in the painting competition either.'

'Even after all these years of teaching,' Harold said, 'I still have to remind myself sometimes that children are just as creative as grown-ups – more so, actually.'

The sun had been shining on and off. It had gone behind a cloud again, but there was a muggy atmosphere inside the tent. As they pushed back the door-flap and stepped into the cooler air, the fête hailer whistled and then settled into a steady hiss.

'This is what you've been waiting for, everybody.'

The announcer went through a tedious list of raffle ticket numbers and the prizes that went with them, while Lena and Harold waited to find out about the pig.

'And, last but very definitely not least, let's see who's taking home the bacon. It was a close-run thing but the winner did better than anybody has since the year before the coronation – eight pins down with the first two balls.' Lena and Harold looked at each other. 'The winner of bowling for the Church Wensley pig, 1963, is… wait for it… eight pins down with two balls…' Harold's heart was thumping. Lena was jumping up and down with excitement. 'You're not going to believe this. We have two record breakers: one took out first five and then three pins; the other took out first six and then two more. The judges have conferred and agreed that the prize goes to Albert Wainwright – six pins with a single ball.'

'Your face!' Lena said to Harold. 'I've never seen such a picture of relief.'

Harold smiled.

They began walking across the field until Lena realised it was later than she had thought. 'I'm going to miss the bus! And it's starting to rain!'

They broke into a run, but when they were almost at the gate, the bus rumbled past on the main road.

The bus shelter was a hundred yards from the gate.

'Never mind the bus. Keep running,' shouted Harold.

By the time they got to the bus stop, the rain was coming down harder.

'Wait in the shelter. I'll fetch the car and take you home.'

Lena did not have time to think about it. As she stepped into the bus shelter, Harold was already jogging away in the rain. Ten minutes later he was back with the car. Lena got in and they drove to her house.

'Come in and dry out,' Lena said. 'You look wetter than the vicar.

Why not stay for something to eat? It won't be prize-winning Victoria sponge but I can manage beans on toast.'

After they had eaten, they sat and talked about the day. 'It was so good to see you happy,' said Lena. 'I have never seen you let go of yourself like that.'

'Thanks to you,' Harold replied. 'It's the most fun I've had in a long time.'

At the end of the evening, Harold got up, saying, 'I ought to be on my way.'

Lena said, 'Why not stay?'

Harold's body tensed. 'You mean…? I don't know… Do you think?'

She took him by both hands. 'Please stay. I want you to.'

The following morning at breakfast, Harold was quiet. He glanced at Lena now and then but each time he lowered his gaze.

Eventually he said, 'According to the Bible…'

'The Bible,' Lena replied. 'The Bible.'

They looked into each other's eyes and then, with a brief sigh, almost a sob, Harold got up. As he went out of the door, he said, 'I'm sorry.'

Lena smiled sadly and watched him walk to his car and drive away.

16

Tim and Simon sat side by side against a stack of straw bales in a field of stubble and watched the colour drain from the scene as the evening light faded. They had heard the rumours about why Peter Salt had suddenly left the village; they had seen what happened if you acted on your feelings for other men and got found out.

'Do you think it would be fair if the other person got let off?' Tim asked.

'Not really. They were both doing the same thing. They wouldn't get let off anyway, would they? Not once the police were involved.'

Tim did not reply. He could not shake off the guilt he felt about what had happened to Peter. Tim was the one who had initiated things. And he could not tell Simon he had been unfaithful to him. The realisation surprised him: he had not thought about it as being unfaithful until now.

The conversations the boys had had, and their behaviour, revealed their tacit assumption that they would always be together. They talked often and at length about their future, but not like lovers planning for a closer union. When they talked about being together in the future, they were merely assuming the continuation of the status quo. They had always been together. But despite their close attachment to each other, and their physical expression of it, they had never discussed their sexuality.

An hour earlier they had been looking for pictures in the clouds – mountains and lakes, rocky coasts and tranquil seas. They had been dreaming of life together on some distant island – there, that snow-capped mountain sloping to a coppery strand that could be a beach, with blue-green waters flecked with gold. In the picture they conjured from the clouds, a copse of trees growing almost at the high-water mark stood against the skyline, and close by in a clearing was the place where they would build a house. There was a jetty where they would tie up the boat they would need to dive for shell fish on the coral reef across the bay. Welcome visitors could use it, too. For unwanted visitors there would be a special harbour on the darker side of the island, surrounded by reefs and open to the full force of the tropical storms that would sweep that way. A treacherous path would meander up the cliffs, and at each perilous turn there would be a half-obliterated sign, seeming once to have spelled 'Welcome'.

Now the sky was dark and they sat in silence.

Simon shivered.

'Are you cold?' Tim asked.

'No. Somebody walked over my grave.'

Tim put his arm round Simon's shoulder and nibbled his ear gently. He would have liked to tell him that he loved him, and to have asked him why he seemed so sad. But he knew why. Even though their intimacy had become more than a passing adolescent pleasure, now the bond between them was fading. If it did not fade there was a danger it could transmute into an obligation, instead of a bit of fun between devoted friends.

'Look at the stars,' Tim said. 'They'll be gone soon if the clouds come over from the west. I wonder how far away that one is.'

He did not point at the one he meant, but it did not matter. They were all beyond reach.

'If one of them did get let off,' Tim began again, 'or if he wasn't identified, he'd still be to blame. It would be his fault the other one had got into trouble and been made to suffer.

Especially if it was somebody he was supposed to care about.'

'Dunno how far it is to the stars,' said Simon, still scanning the sky. 'Millions of miles, I suppose. Hey! A shooting star! There's another one! It must be the time of year.'

'How do you mean?'

'Isn't there supposed to be a time of year when you get a lot of shooting stars?'

'I didn't think this was it.'

'P'raps not.'

'I like being in the fields at night. Do you remember how we used to be frightened to go along the path against the beech hedge when there wasn't any moon? I still think it's a bit spooky there – but not here. Away from people it feels safe.'

The boys stood up, put their arms around each other, and kissed gently, affectionately.

From over near the woods came a sharp, haunting cry. The boys ended the kiss and stared into the darkness.

'A fox.'

'It's like it's calling us.'

'Come on, then. Let's go for a walk in the dark.'

17

From the first time that Lena Goschalk had joined the musical group at Harold Prentice's house, the character of the group had started to change. With her presence the atmosphere had become more light-hearted. Maybe it had been to do with the balance of the sexes; maybe it had been to do with Lena's happy-go-lucky approach to life.

Peter Salt's ignominious departure from the village was a blow to the remaining trio. They met as they had planned, the week after he left, but the music-making was an effort rather than a pleasure. All three of them were relieved when the evening came to an end.

Harold went with Lena to the door, but instead of opening it, he hesitated.

'Actually, if it's not inconvenient – it is rather late but I was wondering if you could spare a few minutes?'

'I'm not in any hurry, Harold. Is it about Peter?'

'You'd better come back into the front room.'

Earlier the room had been filled with the sounds of music-making. Its stillness now, when Harold closed the door, made the moment feel too intimate – almost indecent. Even the steady tick of the grandfather clock in the hallway did not penetrate through the heavy door. Harold did not suggest that they sit down. He had never been shy but as he stood back a little from Lena, directed his eyes down to the carpet and spoke almost inaudibly, he gave the appearance of being so.

'Tonight has not been the happiest of occasions but I hope you won't stop visiting us.'

The fire had diminished to an even layer of bright red, glowing coals. He moved towards the companion set with the intention of using the poker to help them die down for the night, the way he did at the end of every evening. But he stood looking at the poker, undecided on whether to pick it up.

'More than that, actually.'

He paused, and coughed.

Then, in a rush of words, he said, 'Would you consider marrying me?'

All she said was, 'Harold!'

They looked at each other awkwardly. Harold searched for the right words to apologise.

Then Lena said, 'I'd been thinking it would have to be me. I've been putting it off.' Harold looked at her questioningly. 'Nineteen sixty-four. It's a leap year.'

It took a few moments for Harold to understand the relevance of this.

'You mean "yes"?'

'Yes.'

'I kept wondering if the real reason you liked coming here might be…' He paused and cleared his throat again. 'I didn't know if it was just a one-off… a spur of the moment thing… after the fête… if I took advantage. I thought you might say "no".'

Lena smiled. 'I was afraid you'd think I was too pushy if I took the initiative. Or else it would look as though I was after a sugar daddy.'

'Do you mind if we tell Melanie? I'm sure she'll be pleased.'

'Don't you think it would be better to wait until the two of you are on your own?'

Harold called Melanie through from the kitchen. 'We've got something to tell you.' There was obvious delight in the way he spoke. 'I just asked Lena to marry me.'

He smiled at Lena and then at Melanie.

'She's agreed.'

Melanie looked bewildered for a moment, before she congratulated them both. There was an awkward pause, and Harold sensed that Melanie and Lena wanted to talk. He made an excuse and went off into the kitchen.

Lena looked compassionately at Melanie. 'Harold shouldn't have been in such a hurry to tell you.'

'It's all right – really it is.'

'...When we've only just found out how Peter misled you.'

Melanie glanced over her shoulder, and closed the door. 'To be honest it isn't a loss – more a relief. I wouldn't wish Peter any harm – he's a lovely man. He doesn't deserve to be treated the way he has been. The truth is, I was looking for a way to break off from him. For my own reasons.'

She looked across at a book of selected songs by Schubert, still lying on top of the music cabinet. She remembered the evening he sang *Winterreise* and thought of the bleak, lonely journey he was facing now.

'It's dreadful how he's been treated.'

'He shouldn't have been driven out of the village,' Lena said. 'It's not as if he was doing anybody any harm... That didn't come out right. I meant, I don't see why men going with men is so terrible – not if it's in their nature. It was wicked of him to deceive you the way he did. It must really have hurt you.'

'And with boys – they say.'

'What do they call boys? Six-year-olds? Of course. Twelve-year-olds? Yes. Nineteen-year-olds...? The law calls them all children if they're not twenty-one. Not that it stops the younger party being branded a criminal as well. I don't believe they were "boys" the way the word makes it sound. I bet they knew what they wanted.'

Melanie glanced at Lena and then looked away, fiddling

with a loose thread on her sleeve but paying no attention to it, her eyes directed towards the corner of the room.

'You mustn't put the blame on him for leading me up the garden path,' she said. 'We were sort of walking up the garden hand in hand.'

She studied Lena's face, trying to see if her hint had been understood, but she could not tell.

'I should have stood up for Peter. Me, of all people.'

18

It was the spring mid-term break, and Tim and Simon had taken an afternoon off from revision to walk across the fields to a favourite spot. They sat in the branches of an oak tree, with their legs dangling, and talked about some of the things they had got up to in their childhood. After a while they fell into silence.

Simon eventually spoke again. 'Do you remember Lipstick Len?'

'Who?'

Simon shifted his weight to escape the pressure of a nodule of bark under one leg.

'Len Somebody – he lived up Back Lane, near the Toll House – you know, in that house sideways on to the road that didn't have electricity for ages.'

'I thought Watkinsons lived there.'

'They do now. I mean before that. I was going up the lane with Ruth. I remember I'd got new shoes and they'd given me a blister on my ankle. I must have only been seven. This bloke came the other way. I don't know if I was hobbling a bit, but Ruth told me to walk properly and make it look as though we knew where we were going. "Keep close to the side," she said. "It's Lipstick Len – he might get you." When he came by there was a smell of perfume and you could see he was all made up – lipstick and stuff. It wasn't a flowery perfume – more sort of woody – but perfume all the same.' He pulled a face to show his distaste.

'He was wearing a yellowy-brown suit that showed things up a bit, if you know what I mean. Ruth said he was "one of them". The way she said it, it sounded conspiratorial, as though I ought to know what it meant. I didn't, of course. Well, perhaps in a vague sort of way. I don't imagine she did either. She'd just got it from somebody.' He shifted his leg again, which was still pushing up against the nodule of bark, and rubbed it with one hand.

'I suppose he was…' Simon continued, 'you know.'

Tim put his finger in front of a ladybird creeping along the branch he was sitting on and persuaded it to climb onto his hand. He watched her walking across the back of it and then onto his other one, as he moved them around in response to her meandering progress.

'Dunno,' Tim replied. 'I've never seen anybody made up like that. Except on the stage. My dad says there's a lot of it in actors. He says he thinks they're women in men's bodies.'

'I don't ever want to be like that.'

'Nor me. I like being a man. It's men's things I like.'

Simon said, 'You know that page in the paper where people who want advice send their problems in? Somebody wrote in to ask how it happens. Apparently, men like that turn you queer if they get to you when you're young enough. The same as getting hooked on drugs. Everybody goes through a phase, but they know how to trap you in it. You never grow up properly.'

The conversation stopped for a while. Simon gazed across the fields at a plume of smoke coming from a bonfire behind some farm buildings on the skyline. Tim went on playing with the ladybird until it spread its wings and flew away.

'We ought to give it up, now we're getting older,' said Simon.

When they were together, no matter what they were doing, Simon's thoughts were dominated by how much he wanted Tim. When they were apart, he was obsessed with his desire to be with him. He could not imagine how his love for Tim could change. But he was still young. It was not too late. He needed to be resolute.

Tim said, 'We'll be going away to university soon… P'raps just for a few more weeks…'

They climbed down out of the tree and tunnelled into a nearby tangle of rhododendron bushes.

19

Lena and Harold decided they would wait until the last Saturday in July for their wedding. It was long enough after the end of term to give them time to unwind, and still early enough in the summer holiday for them to enjoy a honeymoon without starting to worry about the new school year.

They discussed ideas for the honeymoon one day while Melanie was out shopping. They did not feel comfortable talking about it in her presence.

Somewhere exotic would have been nice, but trips to places like Madeira were all booked up. It might have been too hot, anyway, at that time of year.

'What about Scotland?' Harold asked. 'I've not been for a long time.'

'It's beautiful when the weather's right. Come to think about it, that needn't matter. Pouring rain day after day is miserable on the bike, but if we were in the car, stormy weather over the mountains would be dramatic. I'm not sure about the beginning of August, though. Scotland will be full of midges and caravans in equal numbers.'

America was supposed to be the glamorous choice, but it was ruled out because of the expense and because Harold had seen too much that he disliked about it on the television. In the end they decided in favour of Austria, and Harold telephoned the travel agent to book a ten-day stay in Innsbruck.

The wedding itself would be a simple one, with just a few close family members and friends. With the honeymoon settled, there was little more about the near future to worry about. Plans for what would happen after their return were not so easy. Should they live in Harold's house, or Lena's? Harold's house was more pleasantly located and big enough for all of them. Lena's was more convenient for getting to and from school but it was much smaller.

'If we live in your house,' Harold said, 'I don't think Melanie will want to come with us. It would leave her rattling around a bit in this place but she's very attached to it. On the other hand, if we stay here, she might feel obliged to move out herself. I wouldn't want her to have to do that. I know you get on well with Melanie, but taking on a grown woman as a stepdaughter is not like taking on a child. We might start wanting the place to ourselves anyway.'

'Why don't we leave it till after we get back?' Lena suggested. 'Then we can discuss it properly. She might have ideas of her own by then. We can all live here to start with and see what she decides. I'd like a bit of time to sort one or two things out myself.'

'I've been wondering if we could persuade Melanie to stay with the Hollingworths while we're away,' said Harold. 'Rather than being on her own.'

Lena nodded towards the window. 'She's coming in. Anyway, I think there's an alternative…'

'Goodness, it's busy in town today,' called Melanie as she closed the front door behind her. 'At least I got everything.' She went into the kitchen to put things away, and it was not long before sounds came through of her getting the tea ready.

Lena joined her. 'What needs doing?'

'Thanks. It's nothing special. I got some pyclets in town. The grill should be hot enough. Can you start toasting them while I mash the tea?'

Lena ducked her head a little to peer at the grill, to make sure it was glowing red. 'I was wondering if I could ask you a favour,' she said. She loaded the grill pan and pushed it under the heat. 'I promised to go to Wales with Ruth Hollingworth in the school holidays but obviously I can't do that now. I don't suppose you could take her?'

Melanie was about to put the lid onto the teapot. She gazed at the circulating tea leaves.

Lena continued. 'Not camping in Wales – I can't see you doing that – but if you could take her out on a few day trips…?'

'Why not camping?' Melanie replied, putting the teapot lid in place. 'I used to, years ago. I was quite adventurous in the days before mother died. I backpacked all the way to Athens once – and I went camping in Norway. You know how it can rain in Norway! I don't think Wales would be a problem.'

She put the teapot onto a tray alongside the sugar bowl and a milk jug, took a bottle of milk out of the fridge and filled the jug.

'I'm not sure about the tent though,' Melanie said. 'It's an old-fashioned thing compared to the ones you see these days.'

'Borrow mine,' Lena replied. 'It sleeps two. I shan't be needing it for the honeymoon, I should hope. Ruth knows how to put it up. What about cookers? There's a choice – Primus or gas?'

'If you're sure you don't mind. I always felt camping gear was a bit personal.'

'I wouldn't offer if I minded.'

Melanie lifted her shoulders and her face lit up in a way that Lena had rarely seen.

'I thought I was past doing outdoor things but I'm getting excited already!'

But as she picked up the tray, ready to carry it through to the dining room, her face became serious again.

'Aren't we rather making assumptions?' Melanie asked. 'I

can't see Ruth wanting to go with me, when she was supposed to be riding on the back of your motorbike. She must think I'm awfully boring.'

Lena shrugged, with a deliberately casual shake of her head. 'I'll ask her – oh damn! Excuse the language – the pyclets.'

She pulled them out from under the grill, but it was too late.

20

That year the summer came and went faster than it had ever done. Tim and Simon had found themselves shut up inside for a large part of it to struggle with statistics and the writing of literary criticism. Even the wait for the examination results seemed short as they occupied themselves with day trips on their bicycles, or strolled between the fields of sun-bleached barley rustling in the warm air. They both did well, as they had secretly known they would, and their places at university were assured. They had chosen where they wanted to go months before. They had never discussed going to the same place – tacitly understanding that it was time for them to split up.

At the end of September, they were together near the wood. The barley and the wheat had been harvested and the fields were waiting for a new beginning.

Both of them had grown into young men with looks that caught people's attention.

Tim might have won the leading role in a romantic film if he had chosen that course. He would have been extrovert enough, too. He was a little taller than average but not lanky the way men of eighteen can be. He had broad shoulders and hypnotic blue-grey eyes. As he stood among the corn stubble, straight-backed, his feet slightly apart, he could have been modelling for an advertisement for men's clothing. His smartly cut and carefully groomed black hair framed a square-chinned, pink face – softly pink, not red or weather-worn – with a broad forehead. He already had a strong growth of black beard that cast a dark shadow over his lower cheeks, upper lip and chin, even when he was closely shaved. There was not a blemish on his skin.

Simon had always caught people's attention but not because he was handsome – at least, not in any conventional way. As he matured, he had become more and more like a hero cut straight from a comic book – short, improbably bright, tangerine hair that crowded his head like the spines of a brass wire brush; deep set, amber eyes in a face showered with golden freckles and so full of angles that it might have been the defining style of a graphic artist; a small, neat, muscular body. As he stood facing the impressive figure of Tim, he might have been squaring up for a comic-book fight, were it not for the poignant way they looked into each other's eyes.

In the morning, Tim would get on a train to Cambridge and Simon's father would drive him to Manchester.

'Are you going to join the climbing club?' asked Tim.

'I think I might try caving as well.'

'Ugh. You're welcome to that. I'll see you at Christmas, then.'

'If I come home,' said Simon. 'I'll miss you but I suppose that is how life has to be.' It was not how he wanted life to be. What would the purpose of existence be, living without Tim? It was what was expected of him. It was time to venture into adult life and seek a wife. 'I'll miss you' was the most he could allow himself to say.

Tim moved closer to him and they kissed.

'What's Ruth going to do?' asked Tim.

'Haven't you heard? She's going around with Melanie Prentice. She's got a job as a dumper truck driver at the quarry.'

'She always was a bit of a tomboy.'

'S'pose she was.'

21

The view through the square bay window of a little council house in Fallowfield was of a street like a thousand others across England, lined with small plane trees and littered with cars. A lanky busy Lizzie stood on the window ledge, along with a couple of slightly faded, black and white photographs of a smiling young man in football gear, and a silver cup. Simon noticed the reflection of his own freckled face and apricot hair, distorted by the curved side of the cup.

He watched his father drive away into the mist and then smiled self-consciously at his new landlady.

'Do you want topping up?' asked Mrs G, waving the teapot.

'No thanks.'

'Sit yourself down and I'll clear away. Robin should be here in a minute.' She continued her conversation in bits and pieces as she went back and forth to the kitchen at a lively pace that belied her seventy years. 'What do you think of Manchester?'

'I haven't seen it yet. I don't even know how to get to the university.'

'That's easy,' said Mrs G. 'If you get a bus from the top of the road, they all go there. Turn left. The stop on the right isn't any good. Just ask guard to put you off.' Mrs G glanced through the window. 'Here's Robin.'

A round-faced young man, of average height and only slightly overweight, wearing horn-rimmed glasses, was coming along the street, his long black hair trailing onto his shoulders from under a deerstalker. So this was to be Simon's roommate. He came up the path, let himself in and stuck his head round the living room door.

'Howdy,' he said, and disappeared again to take his things upstairs, leaving the door ajar. Within a minute he came back into the room. 'You must be Simon. Come on, I'll take you to the Freshers' Fair.'

'I was going tomorrow.'

'What's wrong with tonight? Come on.'

'Robin,' said Mrs G, 'sit down. You're hardly through the door. Don't you want some tea?'

'My mother's been stuffing me silly all vac. Get your coat, Simon.'

The two men walked up the street through the chill, smoky air and took the first bus that came along. They alighted at a street corner, walked between some university buildings and went into the one that housed the Students' Union. The place was poorly maintained and smelt of stale beer, but what struck Simon were the clamour of people all his own age, and the uninhibited posters about all manner of things on every square inch of wall. Robin led the way to a room where tables were set out promoting the many clubs and societies.

He abandoned Simon, saying, 'You'll find me in the bar upstairs.'

Simon suddenly felt very alone. He was used to going everywhere and doing everything with other people – usually with Tim. He had read the list of societies in the literature he had received before he left home, and he knew which ones interested him, but it was bewildering to see the choice spread out in the hall. He wandered round, looking at the stands and wondering at their number and variety. Who would join the Tiddlywinks Society, or the Silly Hats Brigade?

He found the Christian Union, put his name down for membership and was invited to a welcome meeting scheduled for the weekend. Speaking to the club representatives and signing up made him feel less of an outsider, and he crossed to the Climbing Club stand more confidently. Another fresher, with short, black hair, dark eyes and smooth, brown skin, was signing on.

'What course are you on?' asked Simon.

'Chemistry.'

'First year?'

'Yes.'

'So am I.'

'How much have you done?'

'Chemistry?'

'Climbing.'

'Hardly any.'

'Nor me.'

'I'm Simon.'

The other fresher hesitated slightly. Pointing with his pen at his name on the form he was filling in, he said, 'Oh, yes, right. Gupta… George Gupta.'

The two of them completed the formalities of joining the club and went together to the bar upstairs. They did not go over to Robin, who was in riotous conversation with three other students standing at the far end of the room and barely visible through the crowd. George drank orange juice and Simon ventured to drink half a pint of beer. Ill at ease, they held a fragmented conversation well away from the bar, jostled from time to time by people coming and going.

Simon looked unwaveringly into George's face. It was something he often did when he was talking to a man. He might give himself away if he allowed his gaze to roam over a man's body. It was a round face, with soft-looking cheeks beneath large, kindly eyes. It did not occur to Simon that being stared at might make George uncomfortable. George looked down at his drink most of the time. Whenever he looked up and their eyes met, he averted his. Simon fancied, at these moments, that George's eyes traced a hurried scan of his body before they caught his gaze, but he did not risk responding by looking George up and down in a similar way.

By the time they parted at the end of the evening, they had taken a liking to each other but had volunteered nothing of consequence about themselves. Simon was aware that George was neatly dressed and that his clothes were in perfect accord with his body. He had registered none of the details, having controlled so carefully where he directed his eyes. His first impressions of George came only from what appeared to be written on his face: how vulnerable he looked and how in need of affection; how much he seemed to be as lonely as Simon felt.

22

Simon went to the Christian Union meeting he had seen advertised, for the welcome talk from one of the lecturers, on the following Sunday.

The speaker's delivery was uninspiring. It was as spiritless as his appearance, despite his efforts to affect enthusiasm. He rambled on about coming into the wide world, about the privileges and opportunities of being in Manchester, about the university and the city. It was fortunate that Simon and the people around him did not need to be told how exciting their new life was, because, for all his efforts, the man exuded unalloyed despondency. He said that he would end on a serious note, apparently thinking that what had gone before was light-hearted.

'Most of you are living away from home for the first time, and you will find your new freedoms confusing. Remember the standards that your parents have taught you. It is easy to slide into loose morals – especially in matters of personal relationships. Just a couple of weeks ago a young black student came to me for advice. He was from Malawi, where he had led a sheltered family life and been watched over by the teachers at his Catholic school. Bewildered by the seemingly different standards of our culture, he had allowed himself to be enticed into ways he would never have thought of in his own country. This shy young man roamed the shadier streets of Moss Side and suffered the shame of contracting a sexual disease.'

He paused, scanning his audience from face to face, before his concluding remarks.

'Well, I am sure you will all have a very happy time in

Manchester, and that you will look back on it with pride and pleasure. I wish you happiness as you build new friendships. Keep yourselves clean and healthy. Walk in the ways of the Lord… and stay away from homosexuality.'

The students rose from their seats and moved into an adjacent room, where tea and sandwiches were laid out. It had the familiar smell of gas that Simon associated with church halls, emanating from a venerable brass geyser which watered the capacious teapots. He joined in conversation with a group – some of them freshers like himself, some second- and third-year students. He offered a banana sandwich to a girl called Cathy with neat, blond hair and an appealing Lancashire accent who was studying geology.

She had an athletic body but was not overly lean – she was softly-contoured. Her delicate but slightly square jaw gave her almost boyish good looks.

Before he came to university, Simon had hoped to be in lodgings with a handsome man. Other men who craved forbidden intimacy might, like him, choose to share a room. It was a dream that conflicted with his desire to conform to normality, but the allure of men was natural to him. He constantly deliberated over whether something that felt right could be a sin, or whether it might be sinful to stifle it. If fate delivered him a mate with whom to share his love, the moral decision would be made for him.

Fate appeared to have denied him his wishes. Simon felt no attraction to his roommate, Robin. Perhaps his interest in men was waning the way it was supposed to do, now that he was away from Tim, and he would eventually fall in love with a woman. He smiled at Cathy. She responded in kind, and they got into conversation.

She was from Ribchester, and she told him how she used to play among the remains of the Roman baths. Simon mistakenly imagined that parts of them would still be standing, like the walls at Ashby Castle, which he had visited from time to time with his parents. He remembered how the entrance to a dark tunnel from one building to another had lured him underground. He would have climbed the crumbling structures above ground but for the wardens' watchful eyes and his parents' admonitions to heed the prohibiting signs. He had been taught to abide by the finest details of the law.

Something in Cathy's manner suggested that she might be less constrained by rules than he was. Her easy smile, perhaps, or the casual way she pushed a space between the plates for her cup and saucer while she helped herself to sandwiches. He asked her if she climbed on the ruins in Ribchester, rather hoping that she did.

She laughed. 'There aren't any bits high enough. You could step on and off most of the walls that are still there. What's the point of climbing anyway? Getting to the top so that you can come down again.'

'It isn't getting to the top. It's finding the way up. Holding onto the rock.'

Cathy laughed again – a friendly laugh. 'Rock? Walls aren't rock. They're piles of stones.'

'I meant real climbing – on gritstone, limestone...'

'Millions of years and millions of sea creatures. Mountains made of sea shells. It's why I'm doing geology.'

Simon had never given a thought to the history of the rocks he climbed on – he was motivated by the joy of caressing their surfaces. The difference between Cathy's interest in rocks and his could not be greater: the difference between detached observation and fervour. But something that Simon and Cathy did have in common would draw them together – their yearning for companionship.

23

The chemistry laboratories filled Simon with excitement. It was the combination of working with his hands and the potential for dramatic things to happen that had drawn him to chemistry. As his skills in the lab developed, he would be taught how to do experiments that required courage. He would feel the trickle of adrenaline as he melted a high explosive in an analytical test, distilled a deadly-toxic liquid, worked with a mixture that was kept from bursting into flames only by his care in handling it. For now, boiling solutions in alcohol and crystallising strange-smelling substances were thrilling enough.

The students had been put into pairs for practical work. As 'Gupta' fell next to 'Farley' alphabetically, the two new acquaintances were teamed up. Two weeks into the course, they were turning pinacol into pinacolone, to illustrate something obscure about molecular rearrangements that they had not yet understood. The white pinacol crystals that they had made the week before had a clean, minty smell and the pinacolone was similar, but subtler.

Simon watched George's elegant, brown hands deftly fitting together the distillation apparatus and adjusting the flow of steam to the heating bath to get a steady boiling rate. The two men were closely matched in physique: they were about the same height and athletic, not gym-freak muscular but without an ounce of fat on them. George knew how to dress attractively and his clothes were stylish without being formal. In the laboratory he was just another student in a lab coat, but Simon pictured the immaculate clothes beneath, and what George himself might be like within the clothes. When George was not preoccupied with controlling the experiment, his gaze seemed often to dwell on Simon's rust-coloured hair, but if the men made eye contact, they broke it at once.

Taciturn though George was, Simon got him to say a little about his background. He was from Cambridge – a painful reminder to Simon of his lost lover, now in that city. George's parents ran a little shop on Mill Road, on the same side of the city as Marshall's airport. Simon did not even know that Cambridge had an airport. He had a vague and inaccurate idea of where Cambridge was, placing it in the rambling northern suburbs of London – somewhere near the further reaches of the Central Line – and not in a place where an airport might be expected.

'What's it like, being an immigrant?' Simon asked.

'I'm British. I wasn't born here but it's the only place I remember. I don't see myself as an immigrant.'

Simon dipped his head by way of an apology.

'I don't suppose it is as bad as it was for my mum and dad,' George said. 'People have got used to seeing us around, even if some of them do treat us like undesirables.'

George adjusted the flow of steam that was heating the flask of liquid, to slow down the rate at which it distilled into the collecting vessel at the other end of the condenser. He smiled amiably.

'There are miles of countryside between Cambridge and London,' he continued. 'It's only a bike ride from our shop to the bluebell woods on the Gog Magog Hills.'

'I thought Cambridge was flat. I've always imagined it as so flat that if you dropped a marble it wouldn't go anywhere.'

'Don't get too excited. When you've struggled to the top of the Gogs you're still only two hundred and forty feet above sea level!'

Sharing the amusement, the two men felt able to look straight into each other's eyes for the first time since the conversation had started. Simon felt an emptiness – a longing. They turned their attention back to the experiment they were doing, as George transferred the fragrant liquid that he had distilled to a sample tube.

'Couldn't you get into the university in Cambridge?' Simon asked.

'You have to pass a Latin exam.'

Earlier in the conversation, George had said he had been to the Perse School in Cambridge. He had described it as a school with an impressive reputation, stretching back centuries.

Simon said, 'You must have done Latin at school. Even we did. Mind you, it didn't interest me much. I suppose you were the same? I dropped it after a year.'

'How can you take a university seriously if it thinks you have to know Latin to be any good at chemistry? Anyway, as you were just saying, Cambridgeshire's flat. Cambridge is as far from climbing as you can get without falling in the sea. Unless you climb the buildings – some people do that – at night, to avoid getting caught.'

'All the same – a Cambridge degree.'

'There isn't even any point in going out walking. You don't exactly get the feeling of adventure standing in the middle of a field of sugar beet.'

'You'd have been better off living at home. The grant doesn't leave much once you've paid for digs.'

Simon sensed that there was more to it – wanted there to be more to it. He would have continued the interrogation but, sensing that George might close up altogether, he dropped the subject.

24

Although Cathy did not share Simon's interest in rock climbing, they both missed the countryside and so they decided to go out by train for walks in the Peak District. They went to Bakewell one Saturday to explore the nearby dales. It was warm for the time of year – perhaps it would be the last warm day of the season. The grassy path across the fields out of Bakewell was wet but not muddy and it glistened in the slanting sunshine.

They were so taken with Bradford Dale that, instead of leaving it earlier where they intended to, they crossed the river and walked upstream. Where the path was wide enough, they walked side by side, hand in hand; where it was narrow, they walked one behind the other, still holding hands. When they came to a bridge, they crossed the river and began the return on the other side. As they walked through the edge of Youlgreave, Cathy commented that she would like to come back in the spring to see the well dressings – pictures with biblical themes made by applying flower petals to moist clay on boards.

'I've never seen them,' Simon said.

'What? And you living so near? Even I've heard about them.'

'Nobody suggested coming when I was little as far as I remember. It's not the sort of thing I'd have come to see on my own when I got old enough to ride this far on my bike.'

They took a path across the fields, away from Youlgreave now, and followed it until they reached Lathkill Dale, almost at its head. After they had been walking down the dale for about a quarter of an hour, they came to a place where the river emerged from a cave on the opposite side of the valley. They sat on a rock beside the path to eat their packed lunches, enjoying the warmth of the sun and the gentle sounds of the river as it flowed smoothly between the stones and through the trailing water-weed.

Having finished, they got up to leave, but Simon wanted to peer into the resurgence cave first. Cathy was reluctant to crawl into the wet vegetation beside the cave mouth and so he left the pack that he was carrying for both of them where it was beside her and went to the cave entrance by himself.

'Don't go in,' she said.

'You can't,' said Simon. 'Only when it's dry and the river stops flowing. I only want to see.'

The roof was low but there was a small space above the water. It looked intimidating, but in some way inviting at the same time, and it set him to thinking that he should go out with the caving club soon.

As he got up he noticed how clear the water was and saw, in the bottom of the shallow stream, a stone that looked as though it might be quartz with a few crystals of lead ore in it. He leaned in to reach for it, oblivious to the slipperiness of the wet ground, and fell sideways into the stream. The water was only a few inches deep, but the right side of his jumper and half his T-shirt were soaked.

He took hold of the stone that had caught his attention, picked himself up and, laughing, stumbled across to Cathy. 'The things a man will do for a woman. Here, have a bit of lead ore.'

Cathy, laughing with him, took the stone and looked at it. 'That's not galena,' she said.

'What is it then?' Simon asked.

Cathy chuckled. 'I don't know either! But it's not lead ore – I'd say it was quartz with a black bit in it.'

'Very technical.'

'Poor you. You're all wet.'

'Only down one side. Anyway, it doesn't matter. I brought a spare T-shirt in case it rains, and a spare jumper.'

He opened the top of the day-pack and pulled them out. He stripped off his wet jumper and T-shirt, exposing his smooth, muscular torso, and leaned forward to put them into the pack.

'Wait a minute,' Cathy said.

She took the discarded T-shirt from him and used the dry half of it on the wet half of Simon, wiping his arm and then patting gently on his side, back and chest. It was the closest physical contact Simon had ever had with a woman. She gave him a playful prod to the stomach. There was something provocative about the sensation it produced but it was an intimacy that was not natural to him. The contact was disturbing rather than pleasurable, and he backed away.

'That's it,' she said. 'Put the dry ones on while I do the bag.' She passed his spare clothes over to him, pulled everything else out of the day sack, squeezed what water she could from the wet jumper and T-shirt, packed them in the bottom of the sack and put the rest of the things on top. Then she ran her hand down Simon's newly clothed arm and briefly linked her fingers with his.

'Better?'

It was another moment of contact that made Simon uncomfortable but, letting his hand fall away, he just said, 'Better!'

'You've not got a poppy.'

It was early November and almost everybody was wearing a commemorative poppy, but not Simon.

'I don't agree with it.'

'All those people who laid down their lives for us…'

'They didn't.'

Picking up the day sack, he continued, 'Poppies are there to allay the discomfort of the people who stayed at home. The soldiers didn't lay down their lives. They were sent to be killed.'

'Is that really what you think?'

Simon realised how opinionated his comments must make him look and wished he had not been so outspoken. Everything about his relationship with Cathy felt awkward.

But Cathy became pensive and said, 'We do set up victims. It seems to be human nature. Sacrifices. Outcasts.'

She gave Simon a penetrating look.

As they continued their walk along the dale, he changed the subject to their plans for after graduation. They both hoped to do PhDs and build careers in academia. Simon wanted to do research. It was what he had wanted ever since he had first thought about adult life when he was a child. Cathy said her ambition was to get into university teaching.

'What's research like in geology anyway?' Simon asked. 'Lots of field trips?'

'That's what got me interested,' said Cathy. 'I love exploring. I could imagine spending my life out and about but the truth is not that romantic. There's a lot of laboratory work, messing about with samples and probably not discovering anything earth-shattering. Teaching must be so much more satisfying.

'In any case, you can't be out on field trips all the time if you have little children to look after. You're bound to end up doing the boring jobs that keep you near to home. But I can't see how teaching could ever be boring.'

'You want to have children then?'

'Most people do, don't they?'

'You wouldn't have to give up travel completely – once they got past being babies – as long as you had a husband who didn't mind looking after them when you were away.'

'Like you.'

Simon gave an evasive half-smile. Turning his face away from Cathy, he pointed ahead of the mill buildings either side of them, to the curve uphill in the road.

'This will be where we go up to Over Haddon.'

The climb was steep, but once they were through the village, it was an easy walk by road and path back to the station in Bakewell. They arrived barely five minutes before the next train to Manchester was due and they took it, in preference to going for tea and hanging around for the next one.

Cathy was in digs near Belle Vue Zoo. Simon accompanied her from Central Station to the trolley bus stop. As the bus came in, she hugged him.

'Thanks for a lovely day out.'

She pulled him closer and kissed him. Simon held her hesitantly and responded as best he could, but his lips remained closed.

The conductor was already ringing the bell. Cathy let go of Simon and jumped onto the bus as it started to move away.

'Bye,' Simon called after her.

He watched the trolley bus depart and waited until the clicks and whines in the overhead wires faded to nothing. A few sparks fell from the ends of the booms when they crossed a junction in the network, and the bus rounded a bend and disappeared. Simon walked back to the stop for his own bus in Piccadilly, imagining what life with Cathy would be like if it were to happen. Why was it so hard to feel the way other men did about women?

25

Mrs G and Robin were not intentionally uncaring – on the contrary, Mrs G positively fussed over Simon – but sometimes their reactionary attitudes frightened him. He came home one evening to liver and onions with a huge pile of mashed potatoes, carrots and processed peas. He struggled to eat it all. He felt run-down and had no appetite – he never had liked liver – but he did not want to worry his landlady. She had noticed that he was unwell and insisted he had a glass of Guinness each night, which she assured him was the ultimate cure-all.

Simon listened to the weekly Wednesday-evening lament from Mrs G's sister. Mrs G's grand-nephew was constantly in trouble with the law, and her sister would come to the house in tears to report his latest misdemeanours. Mrs G blamed the Catholics, the Jews, the 'darkies'. She and her sister reminisced about a time when Moss Side had been a neighbourly place, where people in the narrow, blackened streets knew each other and called greetings across the cobbled passages between the backyards.

Simon was relieved when the sister had her farewell cup of cocoa and went home.

Mrs G explained: 'The council knocked all the houses down and sent her halfway across Manchester. She was right up in a sixth-floor flat with neighbours she'd never met. They might as well have come from Leeds or Newcastle. As soon as they finished the blocks of flats in Moss Side she got a transfer back. The rest of her family stayed in Ancoats. Now she's stuck with a different lot of strangers and not even a street to chat in. Just a lot of concrete monstrosities and empty spaces.'

Robin came breezing in, a little drunk, at eleven o'clock.

'Howdy.'

He slumped into a chair by the fire, pulled out one of his head hairs and started to nibble it.

'Ugh,' said Mrs G. 'Stop that. It's disgusting.'

Robin smiled and carried on.

'Bumped into a poof in Moss Side,' he commented. 'Makes a change from hookers.'

Mrs G clicked her tongue.

'A girl with blond hair sidled up to me and smiled. She didn't say anything and I was just thinking I wouldn't mind bringing her back here…'

'Don't you start bringing loose women into my house,' warned Mrs G.

'Wouldn't be anywhere to take her anyway' – he nodded towards Simon – 'not with him in the bedroom… and then I realised she'd got a five o'clock shadow. It was a fella in drag!'

Mrs G screwed her face up. 'Oh, shut up,' she said. 'I don't want to think about it.

'…Poor bugger,' she added, as an afterthought.

'Well anyway… come on, darling,' Robin jested, taking hold of Simon's hand. 'Time for bed.'

Perhaps he meant no harm, but Simon feared that Robin had suspicions about him. It made him deeply afraid. Men in groups rarely chatted for more than a few minutes without someone making a quip about limp-wristed deviants, but that was because they thought there were none among them. Or was it because the men who made the comments had something to hide?

Robin's remark and action were too deliberate – too knowing. With a slight shake of his head, Simon pulled his hand away.

'Come on,' said Robin. 'I'm knackered. I don't want you blundering in half an hour from now, waking me up, clumping about in the dark.'

They said goodnight to their landlady and went upstairs.

Simon lay in the darkness, longing for Robin to fall asleep. Robin kept talking and talking about nothing that mattered, as he often did. Simon was not paying attention. His thoughts were on a ceaseless orbit around the question at the heart of his existence. How could he live in a world that reviled people like him for an aberration that, try as he might, he could not shake off.

'Didn't he disgust you?' asked Simon when Robin went quiet. 'The bloke in Moss Side?'

'Heck, no. He's just sick, poor sod. Bit of a joke, really.' Robin turned over and seemed to go to sleep.

Soon Simon was asleep too, disturbed by dreams about half-naked men in chains looking down from tower-block windows and crying for freedom and friendship.

26

Just before the end of term, Simon took Cathy home for a weekend. His school chemistry teacher had always counselled forgetting about work for a few days before exams, saying that if you did not know it all by then, it was too late to cram any more in. She claimed never to have revised during her education, and she had got a first-class honours degree. Perhaps she was exceptional – she had chosen to study science at a time when most women stayed at home learning to be neat little housewives – but Simon thought it was sound enough advice.

They travelled on the Saturday morning and arrived in time for a late lunch. The smiles of Cathy and his parents and their glances towards Simon – indelicate hints at his presumed sexual interest in her – embarrassed him. He was not prudish: he was ashamed to be presenting an image at odds with his deepest feelings – signalling falsely to himself as much as to the people around the table.

When they had had lunch, he took Cathy along the path that led beyond the mill and the sluice gates to the spillway. As they watched the water sliding over it, Simon remembered the day Tim had fallen into the pool below. He saw him stumbling towards his mother with tears on his cheeks and water streaming from his clothes, as though his whole body were in tears. The tears came not from fear but from being abandoned – Simon had abandoned Tim, leaving him to flounder alone in the cold water. He recalled what somebody had said on the radio – was it on 'Desert Island Discs'? – 'We're all alone in the end.' Thinking about it now, he wanted to draw the unhappy little boy into his arms and calm him, as Tim's mother had done. He held his hand out to Cathy and they cuddled one another for a few minutes before strolling back to the house.

After spending the evening with Simon's parents, they went to their separate bedrooms at a time that now seemed early to Simon, who was used to keeping student hours. There was a bookshelf in the bedroom, piled high with back-copies of the *Reader's Digest* – too many to stow neatly – and to pass the time he glanced through one or two of them. The triumph over adversity in one was a surgeon saving his unconscious patient in a blazing operating theatre; in another, it was a teenage girl crawling for twenty hours out of the depths of an American cave; then here was one about a vicar who fought and conquered alcoholism; and here – here was a woman who found her husband in bed with another man.

Simon took the book closer to the table lamp, and, sitting on the edge of the bed, began to read.

She had been swept off her feet in a whirlwind romance. The man had serenaded beneath her window one starry, moonlit night, and pleaded for her hand in marriage. Soon after they married, she came home one evening earlier than planned to find the living room empty. She went upstairs. A man she did not know was sitting on the edge of the bed, fastening his shoe. His hair was dishevelled, his shirt was half-unbuttoned and his jacket was lying on the floor. Her husband had his back to the door, but she could see that he was fastening the buckle of his trouser belt. The story went on to describe her horror. Simon read it twice before he got into bed and turned out the light.

Simon and Cathy had agreed, weeks before, that they would go along to the Sunday School that weekend, rather than to the church service. Mrs Hollingworth, who ran the morning class, was more successful at keeping her charges than most Sunday School teachers because of her idiosyncratic treatment of the Bible stories. Simon had promised Cathy that Mrs Hollingworth in action would be immeasurably better than the minister delivering a sermon at the morning service. It was worth going to hear her just to find out what new slant she would bring to a story told a thousand times before.

'I sometimes wonder why we attach any importance to the Old Testament,' Mrs Hollingworth began. 'It is full of violence, cruelty and wickedness. It is very much about a world where the love of God, as we understand it, is hard to find.

'Hard to find, but not impossible. Here and there unsullied love shines out as bright as the brightest star in the blackness of those dark times. And the most perfect example of this is the story of the love between David and Jonathan. If this were a story about a boy and a girl it would be remarkable enough – a story of a poor boy who fell in love with a princess, perhaps, went to her palace and eventually became king. But this is a story of the strong, pure love that can sometimes grow between men…'

When she talked about 'pure love', it was obvious to Simon that she did not see the relationship between David and Jonathan the way he did. Why did she not admit what the story was really about? Was it such a shocking interpretation that even Mrs Hollingworth did not dare to say so – or that she could not believe it? Simon thought about the way the 'pure love' of Ancient Greece had been dismissed or explained away. Was he given to desires so unacceptable that even if they featured in a Bible story and were extolled by the most revered culture in history they were never to be articulated?

When the class had ended with a closing hymn and the children were getting up to leave, Mary Hollingworth came over to Simon and Cathy.

'How nice to see you, Simon.'

She looked enquiringly at Cathy, and he introduced her as one of his student friends.

'Your mother'll be expecting you back for lunch but why don't you come to our house for half an hour and bring Cathy? Ruth'll be there and she would love to see you. She comes round on Sunday mornings with Melanie.'

Melanie, who had been looking after a different group of children in the class, came over.

'Melanie, this is Simon's friend, Cathy. I'm just saying they ought to come back with us and say hello to everybody.'

Simon was uneasy about things that might come out if they went to the Hollingworth's, but there was no easy escape. Even as Mary talked, the four of them were already moving together towards the exit door.

They walked the short distance to the house. Arthur was in the garden, bent over the track of his model railway to make some adjustment to it. He stood up stiffly and led the arriving party into the house. Some bunches of herbs were hung up to dry near the fire, ready to be used at Christmas, and the scent of thyme permeated the room. Ruth was inside. She had anticipated the arrival of the group from Sunday School and already made a pot of tea and put some biscuits onto a plate. Melanie gave her and Arthur each a kiss, lingering, it seemed to Simon, a bit too long over her kiss with Ruth.

Ruth came over to Simon, her eyes sparkling with pleasure, and gave him a brief hug.

'Simon! I'll get two more cups in a minute.'

'Hello, Ruth. This is Cathy.'

Ruth appeared uncertain. She nodded to Cathy and looked back into Simon's face, before turning to Cathy again, greeting her and shaking her hand hesitantly.

'She's at Manchester as well,' Simon continued. 'Doing geology.'

Confronted with Ruth's evident curiosity, he felt obliged to say more.

'I met her at the Christian Union. We both like walking so we get the train into the Peak District on Saturdays. I thought she'd like to see where I come from.'

He wanted to present himself as a normal young man; he wanted to describe Cathy as his girlfriend. But putting it that way would not just be disingenuous; it would be too committing. Even simply introducing her as a friend, he sensed that, from the way Ruth looked at him, she knew he was taking advantage of Cathy.

Arthur came to join them. He had cleaned his hands after coming in from working on his model railway but looked out of place in his tattered old jacket and baggy trousers, surrounded by everyone else dressed for Sunday.

'Getting on all right in Manchester?'

Simon smiled politely but it was a brief, weak smile.

'Cathy, you said, didn't you?' Arthur asked Cathy. 'Don't suppose you're any more interested in trains than Simon ever was!'

Cathy was spared having to answer as the front door opened and Harold Prentice looked in.

'Harold, come and meet Simon's lady friend,' said Arthur. 'It's Ruth's friend's father,' he explained to Cathy. 'Melanie's.' He turned to Simon. 'He's married Lena Goschalk… Was that before you left? It might have been just after.'

Harold came over and shook Cathy's hand. 'Excuse me just for a minute while I say hello to the others.'

Mary Hollingworth was proffering a cup of tea. He went over to accept it and to pick up a biscuit, taking Ruth with him. Simon watched him with Mary, Ruth and Melanie. Harold seemed to be completely at ease. Perhaps he saw Ruth and Melanie as nothing more than good friends.

Arthur was looking at Harold, too. He smiled. 'He's a

different person since Lena took him on. So much happier.'

Harold glanced across and gave a little nod. He made his excuses to the three women and returned to Arthur, Simon and Cathy.

'Are you getting on all right with your studies?' he asked Simon, but he went on without waiting for an answer, turning to Cathy. 'Introduce us, Simon.'

'Oh, sorry,' said Simon. 'Mr. Prentice, this is Cathy. Cathy, this is Mr Prentice.'

'Harold – please call me Harold. Are you taking good care of him, Cathy?' He turned to Simon. 'It's wonderful to see you young folk growing up.' Turning back to Cathy he said, 'I can remember him when he was a little lad in shorts. Such good boys, they were. In the Venture Scouts he was an example to everybody. He's grown into a fine young man. He'll make somebody a splendid husband.'

He paused for a moment.

'Do you see anything of that friend you went around with all the time? I can't think of his name. He wasn't in the scouts... I hope you're keeping in touch.'

Simon stuttered something about not needing to hold onto old connections now that he had started a new life.

Harold adopted his wise elder look. 'Comradeship is so important. The older you get, the more you value the friends of your youth. Once you start having families, you will need each other.'

Simon was with people he had known all his life, people he should belong with but never really had. He glanced at his watch.

'We ought to get back,' he said, looking first at Harold and then at Cathy.

He called to the others. 'Goodbye, everybody.'

Despite his unease, he wanted them to express disappointment and to ask him to stay, but they just called back inconsequentially, 'Bye,' 'Nice to see you,' and went on with their own conversations.

He stepped out of the house with Cathy following him.

As he sat hand in hand with Cathy on the train that afternoon, going back to Manchester, Simon glanced at her, and then turned his eyes away. He watched the telegraph poles speeding past, and the slower procession of distant fields and hedges. A few orange-red rose hips still hung on briars clinging to the slopes of a cutting that grew deeper and deeper, obscuring the far view and eventually even the sky.

'There's something I have to tell you.'

The train entered a tunnel with a sound like someone thumping two big pillows together. Their ears popped and the clatter of the wheels echoed from the walls.

'Go on,' Cathy half-shouted back.

'It's about…'

'Oh, wait,' she interrupted. 'Watch. This side. Any second… There!'

For a brief moment the train broke out into daylight before it plunged into another tunnel. As it did, it crossed high over a tree-filled, limestone gorge in which a quietly flowing river caught the last light of the day. It was like seeing a wonderful photograph flashed onto a screen for just a second – long enough for its beauty to thrill the watcher; gone too soon.

'Isn't that marvellous? I watch out for it every time we come this way.'

Simon sat in silence, gazing at the floor.

'Simon, what's wrong?'

'I'm sorry,' he said, 'but it isn't going to work.'

Cathy gave a little smile of the kind that is more for self-reassurance than for the onlooker. It faded to leave her face empty and waiting. As they came out of the tunnel, Simon noticed the grubbiness of the upholstery of the seat opposite him, the dinginess of the yellow-brown panelling above it. Despite the intermittent rain outside, his nose and throat felt dry from the dusty, sooty-smelling air in the compartment.

'It isn't anything to do with you. You're a really nice person. It's me. I like having you as a friend, but I don't want you to think it's leading to marriage, or anything.'

'Simon, you poor thing…'

'I don't believe I can ever really love anybody. Not – you know – passionately.'

'Simon, that's awful.'

'It's just how I am.'

Inside, Simon knew how much he really could love. He was barely able to contain his grief over his separation from Tim. There was no resolution to the contradiction he constantly returned to in his mind: it felt natural and right to him to give his love to another man and yet it filled him with shame. He could not tell anyone if he wanted to stay part of his communities and on the right side of the law.

'I'm sorry,' he said, 'I never meant to hurt you.'

'I think I understand,' Cathy said, putting her hand onto the back of Simon's. 'We will stay friends, won't we?'

She burst into tears and he did the same. The train rattled on, carrying its unhappy cargo towards the gloom of a damp, smoky Manchester evening.

27

Tim settled quickly into life at Gonville and Caius College in Cambridge. The environment he found himself in was different in almost every way from the one he had left behind, but that was what he liked about it. The idea of wearing gowns for dinner in the oak-panelled hall, watched over by portraits of dignitaries from bygone times, entertained him. The dons reciting grace in Latin from their raised daïs entertained him even more – especially the one who was incapable of remembering the words and repeated them a few at a time, prompted by a colleague. There was good wine with the meals; he had not been used to that at home!

He missed Simon at first but he soon started to enjoy his independence. Some of the young men in college were liberal-minded and talked casually about same sex relationships, which they saw as moral, respectable – even honourable – whatever the law might say. Within the walls of the college, Tim was open about his liking for men. His immediate friends thought no less of him for it. Indeed, they admired his courage in the face of social hostility, including hostility from some other students, and the threat of legal sanctions. When someone had said to Tim that he was 'in the wrong college', he thought for a moment he was about to hear an insult, but in fact it was said in jest. The speaker went on to say that King's College was allegedly the place to be. Paradoxically, even though none of the students Tim conversed with shared his predisposition, their relationships with him were more relaxed than the ones they had with each other. Perhaps they felt safer talking to him about their disappointments with the young women they pursued.

From his exploits before he left home, Tim knew how to hunt for men, and he quickly discovered the places in Cambridge where they sought each other out. Being in a crowd of like-minded men in the Stable Bar gave him comfort, but the management, ever fearful of the law, had strict rules against displays of affection. Although Tim occasionally found someone attractive who took an interest in him, it never led to anything. Tim was drawn to men more mature than himself, and many of these men were married. They were looking for partners who could take them back somewhere. Tim did not want men from the town nearly twice his age coming to his room. Having other students discover he had smuggled in a male lover would not have worried him – he might even have been pleased to show off his erotic prowess. It was more that the omnipresent sense of exclusivity among the students and their belief in the self-sufficiency of youth would make closeness with a middle-aged townsman embarrassing.

There was, in any case, something thrilling about prowling in the shadows. Tim took to shedding his gown after dinner, changing into casual clothes and doing a round of the most favoured haunts of the hunters and hunted. Towards the end of the evening, he would walk along Jesus Lane to Four Lamps and that was where he most often found what he was looking for.

He did not entirely confine his interests to older men and one evening he slipped into hiding on Midsummer Common with a slim, young man wearing a perfume that mingled cloves and cinnamon, which Tim breathed in as he nuzzled him behind his ears. Usually there was little conversation during Tim's clandestine liaisons on the Common – it was easier to remain incognito if they stayed silent – but on this occasion they chatted more freely. The stranger had a West

Country accent, and this prompted Tim to ask him how he came to be at Cambridge, rightly guessing that he was also a student. The student asked Tim if he was a member of one of the cliques who clustered around dons of a particular bent. Tim had known for years what he had supposed to be a kind of folklore about the goings-on at Cambridge. It was only now that he realised these dons might actually exist.

'I don't go either,' the student said. 'It's all a bit prissy for me. I like this better.'

Conversation ceased as they gave themselves to each other, sliding their hands into each other's clothes. Even out in the cold and damp they found a kind of brief bliss. Then it was over, and they stumbled out of the bushes and went their separate ways. As he turned onto St John's Street, Tim realised he had not asked the stranger who the accommodating dons were. Perhaps he would not have told him anyway.

It was one of Tim's straight college friends who put him onto Donald Wolfcote, through an almost throw-away remark a couple of days later.

'How's things, Tim?' his friend said, sitting down beside him on the bottom of the steps that led down from their rooms, and gazing across the quadrangle at a couple of pigeons pecking at the gravel path.

As he spoke, Professor Donald Wolfcote came out past the porters' lodge into the quad, and walked across the middle of the grass, as senior staff were permitted to do.

'Professor Wolfcote's one of your type, if you know what I mean – or, so I've heard.'

Donald Wolfcote walked briskly with several books tucked under his arm, his gown billowing behind him. His immaculate suit was perfectly tailored to his strong, lean body, the outlines of which could have been those of a man of barely half his sixty-eight years. His kindly face, even though it bore a neatly-cropped, white beard, still had a youthful appearance. He presented it only in profile as he hurried along, but then one of the books he was carrying slipped a little and he directed his attention to it, not looking at the two students but turning his full face towards them.

'Oh, is he?' Tim said, in what he hoped was a dismissive tone. He had not come across Professor Wolfcote within the university but he had seen that face before.

28

During the following week or two, Tim spent more evenings in the Stable Bar than previously and, eventually, Donald Wolfcote turned up. He looked even less like a don in worn jeans and a T-shirt than he had done crossing the quad in his smart suit, when his chalk-marked gown had been the only thing about him in keeping with the stereotype of his profession. He was talking with a group of men, all of whom appeared to be in their sixties and beyond. Perhaps sensing that someone was interested in him, he glanced across the room towards Tim. Their eyes met briefly before Donald turned his attention back to his friends.

Tim watched Donald's animated gestures as he pursued a lively conversation. It was not long before Donald glanced at Tim again and this time his gaze lingered a little. Tim moved to a stool nearer to Donald, choosing a spot directly illuminated by an overhead lamp so that he stood out against the shadowy background. He faced towards him and lounged with one forearm against the bar. Donald's glances became longer and more frequent, but he showed no inclination to break away from his friends and they showed no sign of leaving.

It must have been half an hour before the group of men including Donald finished their drinks and got up to leave. They did not move away from the bar immediately, hanging back to talk with one of the barmen. Donald wrote something down on a small piece of paper. He looked across at Tim and then turned his attention back to his friends. Perhaps he did not want to risk an overt approach in public, even inside a bar like this one. According to the stories Tim had heard, you could be prosecuted just for smiling at another man. He felt no need to be secretive with his student friends inside college, but he knew that outside college the slightest unwise word or action could be his undoing.

He got up, walked over to the door, and waited close to it nervously while Donald and his friends finished their conversation with the barman. Should he follow Donald if he split away from his friends when they exited? He did not know what sort of temperament Donald had. Being pursued into the night by a stranger might be a turn-on for one kind of person; it could be threatening to another – even to one who might have invited a liaison through meaningful glances.

The group were almost at the door. Tim stepped in front of them, feigning to make for the exit without bothering to watch for other people going the same way, and Donald bumped into him.

'Sorry, young man,' said Donald. 'After you.'

He put a hand on Tim's shoulder and steered him towards the door. As he did so, his other hand brushed against Tim's to give him the piece of paper he had written something on a few minutes earlier. Tim took it as inconspicuously as he could and clutched it inside his closed fist. Outside, the men all turned left, and so Tim turned right.

Once he was out of their sight and there was no one else around to see what he was doing, he looked at the paper. He could not read it properly in the dim light, but it was a telephone number.

His first thought was to go straight to a telephone box near the bus station, but it would be frustrating to dial repeatedly, before Donald had had time to reach home, and get no answer. He ought to go back to college and try calling the number the next evening, but that would leave him agitated and impatient through a wakeful night and an inattentive day in the lecture theatres. To kill time, he walked out along Regent Street and turned onto Lensfield Road. Part way along Lensfield Road he caught the sweetish chemical smell that drifted from the chemistry laboratories opposite – not really like warm brown sugar, but somehow akin to it. It set him to thinking about Simon, away in Manchester. He imagined the laboratories there smelt the same and he wondered how Simon was getting on. Their partnership, long though it had lasted, already seemed far into the past, but Tim would have liked to know that Simon was all right.

Reaching Tennis Court Road, he turned back towards the town centre.

When he got there, enough time had elapsed for him to try making the call, but there were already people in both phone boxes on Emmanuel Street. If he walked for a few more minutes, different people would almost certainly take them over, and so he stood and waited until one of the boxes became vacant. Finally he hauled the door open and went in. Why did they all have the same, fusty, vaguely metallic smell? Fumbling with one hand to unfold the piece of paper, with the other he felt among the coins in his pocket for four pennies. He lifted the handset and dialled. The telephone seemed to ring for a long time, and he was about to give up and walk around for a bit longer, when someone answered.

He pushed button A. 'Somebody gave me this number earlier this evening.'

Donald Wolfcote answered. 'You must be the young man with black hair.'

Tim had not paid attention to Donald's voice when he had spoken to him so briefly in the doorway of the bar. He was not quietly spoken, but his voice was gentle, and it had an expressive intonation such as might come from a newsreader on the radio.

'You kept looking at me,' Tim said.

‘I thought it was you trying to catch *my* attention. Was there something you wanted to talk about?’

‘Can I come to see you?’

‘Are you a student?’

‘I’m doing architecture.’

‘Don’t you think you ought to talk to your tutor if you have a problem?’

‘I haven’t got a problem. Well, not really. I just thought you might let me come to see you.’

The line went quiet for a short time and then Donald spoke again. ‘Why don’t you come round tomorrow… oh, wait… Not tomorrow, I’ve got a lot on this weekend. Come round on Monday evening.’ He told Tim where to find his flat, in a building set back from Trumpington Road. ‘Come round after dinner.’

29

The weekend seemed interminable. Saturday dragged on in a way that Tim rarely experienced. He wandered around the shops for a while but he had no interest in buying anything. His jaunt was intended to keep him occupied, but having that sole purpose, it inevitably failed to do so. Even as he browsed the racks of clothes, his mind was on his forthcoming visit to Donald's flat. He thought about taking to the streets and the park in the evening, but he had no enthusiasm for it. He got through Sunday by burying himself in his studies. Little of what he read registered in his mind.

Monday was easier because he had a couple of lectures to attend, and they demanded his full attention. In the breaks between them, student friends drew him into conversation, providing a partial distraction. Towards the end of the afternoon his excitement increased as the time of his assignation approached. His ebullience during dinner prompted two or three colleagues to rag him gently about the date they guessed he must have. He evaded their questions, saying he was just feeling pleased with himself after a good day of study, but he knew his disappearance soon after dinner would be noticed. It had never worried him before that students who witnessed his evening departures might guess the reason, but this time it made him uncomfortable. When he was ready, fresh from a bath and dressed in a cuddly jumper and soft, close-fitting jeans, he checked the landing and staircase were deserted before he slipped out.

He had not expected to feel frightened when he turned into the drive of the house where Donald lived. With shaking hands, he operated the bell push labelled 'Prof D Wolfcote' – relieved to see the name there – and waited, fearing that he might not be welcomed or even that someone different might answer, whatever it said on the label. He heard movement and a silhouette came along the hall behind the frosted-glass window in the door.

Donald Wolfcote led Tim into his ground-floor flat. The high-ceilinged room they entered was comfortably warm and smelt of fresh coffee. The many oil paintings on the walls looked like originals – nearly all of them were impressionist landscapes. Heavy, dark-red curtains hung before the windows. There was a fire burning in the tiled, cast-iron fireplace and two long-haired, blue-grey cats were curled up in each other's arms on a rug in front of it.

Donald gestured Tim to sit down on a soft sofa. It was so soft that it felt like sitting *in* it, rather than on it.

'Want a cup?' Donald asked, waving a coffee pot.

'Thanks.'

'Not many students go to the Stable Bar.'

'No,' replied Tim. Then: 'I like being with men.'

Donald pulled a Queen Anne-style, occasional table out of a nested set in the corner of the room and placed it close to Tim. He stood Tim's coffee on it in an oddly incongruous cheap mug and gave him an affectionate pat on the shoulder. He poured his own coffee and took it to an armchair angled towards the sofa.

He asked how long Tim had known he was drawn to men and whether he regarded it as a problem. Tim replied that his only problem was being under constant threat from the law.

'I knew by the time I was ten. I don't see anything immoral about it – I just like men. I like grown-up men.'

He did not name Peter Salt, nor Simon, but he described having his first sexual experiences with another male almost as soon as he was capable of them, and then went into detail, with a smile, about how, one night in a tent, he had initiated a lasting sexual relationship with a teenage friend. When Tim admitted to meeting strangers in the dark in Cambridge, Donald warned him of the risks: disease, assault, trouble with the law, blackmail.

'It's safer to restrict yourself to the private scene,' he advised.

Tim was not ignorant of the perils of hunting: he was drawn to his precarious night life by the sense of adventure. A mistaken choice of quarry might bring violent retribution, and a lone hunter was prey to men of a different kind – vigilantes filled with hatred who hunted in packs – but heightened levels of adrenaline elevated the pleasures of successful pairings to ecstasy.

He looked around the room, took another sip of the freshly-brewed coffee – a rare treat for him – and felt the embrace of the soft cushions in which he nestled. Such tranquil surroundings were appealing. If they were what Donald meant by the 'private scene' then perhaps, in time, he could find contentment.

From the way Donald looked at Tim, it was obvious that he found him attractive, but it was clear from his courteous behaviour that if Tim wanted to take things further, it would have to be on his own initiation. It reminded Tim of the kind way that Peter Salt had treated him and of the cruel way that others had treated Peter. He wondered if Peter would have had an easier time if he had been a don in Cambridge, or if it was just a matter of luck who escaped maltreatment.

They had been sitting and talking for about half an hour when there was the sound of the front door opening and closing, and a surprised-looking man, perhaps just a little younger than Tim, came into the room.

'Oh, sorry. I didn't know you'd got a visitor.' He turned as if to leave.

'Don't go,' Donald said, and then, to Tim, 'I haven't asked

your name?'

Men who met with men preferred not to exchange names. If one of them got picked up by the police, there would be no names to keep secret. But Tim already knew Donald Wolfcote's name and exactly where he lived. Although this seemed to be an occasion for mutual trust, he limited his reply to his first name.

'Tim.'

Donald gestured politely to the two young men in turn. 'Nalin, this is Tim. Tim, this is Nalin.'

Tim and Nalin gave each other a friendly nod.

'Nalin comes round when he wants a break from the joys of life with his parents.'

'They're trying to get me into an arranged marriage,' Nalin said. He gave a wry smile. 'And they go on about me having too many dodgy honky friends.'

Nalin's arrival might have been an unwelcome intrusion – Tim had been expecting an amorous evening leading to the bedroom door – but making an immediate sexual conquest was becoming less important. Donald would always be there and another attractive man had entered the room. He relaxed and began to enjoy the security of being where he was, with men like himself.

Nalin sat down on the rug in front of the fire with his legs out in front, his forearms on his thighs. One of the cats lifted its head, stretched and moved to lean against him. He ruffled the fur on the back of its neck, and it began to purr.

'Hello, Ben,' he said.

'Ben's the one that likes to be fussed,' Donald said. 'The other one's called Peter.' Alluding to an assumption made by everyone but never expressed, he added, 'They're such good friends I named them after Benjamin Britten and Peter Pears.'

'It's all wrong – arranged marriages,' Tim said. 'If it isn't right for either of them it must wreck the lives of them both.'

'It's the way it is – the culture,' Nalin replied.

They started to talk to each other and Nalin mentioned he worked as a stagehand. For a year or two when Tim was still at school, he and a couple of friends had gone to performances of almost everything put on by the repertory company in the local town. His attendances had become less frequent in his final years because of the pressure of work, but his interest still remained. It was something they had in common that would draw them together.

Nalin was a little shorter than Tim, lightly – almost slightly – built but strong and healthy. He had a neatly trimmed beard and an appealing, good-natured expression. He was not Tim's usual choice in men, but he had the kind of personality that made him immediately likeable to everyone. When Tim left, he took up an invitation to go with him to a performance of a new play called *Loot* at the Arts Theatre.

30

Nalin was waiting in the foyer, holding two tickets, when Tim arrived at the theatre. They joined the crush of people creeping up the stairs, entered the auditorium and settled into their seats.

The fire curtain was down and advertisements for local businesses were being displayed on it. Nalin commented that they might be in the Arts Theatre but the publicity graphics fell a long way short of qualifying as art.

Tim agreed. 'The inapposite claims to deliver reassuring family services would be laughable if they were not so dreary.' He looked at Nalin. 'I didn't ask you what you are reading.'

'Reading? Oh, I see what you mean. I'm not a student.'

'Is this your job then? I'd assumed you were working here part time.'

'Being a stagehand looks like a part-time job to some people, I suppose – especially my dad, who thinks everybody should get up at five in the morning and work until bed time. I mostly work afternoons and evenings. It's six or seven days a week some of the time but then I get a few days off in a row, like now.'

'How do you come to know Donald if you're not a student?'

Nalin hesitated. 'It's a long story. He felt sorry for me and Angela…' His voice trailed away because the lights started to go down.

As the play unfolded, there was much laughter from the audience – none louder or more prolonged than that from Tim and Nalin – but some grunts of disapproval. When the lights went up for the interval, parts of the audience became engaged in merry conversation; others sat in silence, discomfort written across their faces. Perhaps they did not like such aggressive lampooning of the police.

'What do you think?' asked Nalin.

'It's brilliant!'

'That business with the glass eye and the magnifying glass...' Nalin said, and they collapsed into laughter.

'Do you know much about Joe Orton?' Nalin asked.

'Not really.'

Nalin told Tim about Orton's string of letters to the *Daily Telegraph* under pseudonyms and the exploits with library books that had earned him a short spell in prison.

'He and the man he lived with wrote racy blurbs and pasted them over the real ones in the books. I think they even cut out some pages and inserted different ones.'

Tim did not like to appear to be prying but he was more than curious about what Nalin had said before the lights went down. Nalin was not a student and yet he knew Donald – well enough to be entitled to let himself into Donald's flat. The explanation had seemed obvious until Nalin mentioned a woman's name. Now he was happily talking about Joe Orton and 'the man he lived with'. Which way did Nalin's preferences go?

'What was it you were saying about... Angela, was it?'

'My girlfriend. She's gone away with her parents for a week. So I'm at a bit of a loose end.' Nalin noticed the confusion on Tim's face. 'Donald's been really good to us.'

There was another pause before he continued.

'I don't go to Angela's. Her dad's got a thing against immigrants and her mother's just weird. I don't think she'd let her have *anybody* as a boyfriend. Angela doesn't come to my house either. I don't want my dad to know about her. He's decided I'm going to marry one of his cousin's daughters. According to him and his cousin, it's an ideal match. They certainly wouldn't think a white woman was a suitable match – they're as prejudiced as Angela's parents.'

Tim took a breath. He intended to shake off his prior misapprehension about the nature of Nalin's relationship with Donald by expressing some bland comment, but Nalin continued.

'I thought my parents would leave me in peace until my brother was hitched. He's older than me. He's doing chemistry in Manchester and my dad's not going to marry him off until he's got a first-class degree. George is the obedient one. He'll go along with whatever wife my father decides he's getting. It won't even occur to him there could have been anybody better. *I* can't imagine marrying anybody of the sort my dad would choose. I'm keeping quiet about Angela until I've married her and it's too late.'

Nalin glanced around at the people sitting behind them. They were busy with their own conversations. The seats in front, and next to him and Tim, were empty as their occupants had gone to the bar.

'I used to meet her in the Botanical Gardens. My dad had announced he'd found me a wife from what he calls home. When he saw I wasn't falling over myself to agree, he said he couldn't face the disgrace if I refused. It came up day after day – he could keep it going for hours – whole evenings sometimes.'

Nalin shifted in his seat and brushed his dark hair back with his hand.

'I don't see it the same way now, but I decided I was going to have to give in for the sake of family peace. The evening I worked myself up to telling Angela, she was late. On my own on the bench, listening for her footsteps on the path into the gardens, I ended up obsessing over if she was ever going to turn up, how I was going to cope when she did… how I was going to cope if she didn't…'

He paused and brushed his hair again.

'I can't remember if I was actually crying but I was certainly looking miserable. Donald was walking along the path and he noticed. He came and sat next to me and asked what was wrong. He didn't look at me. He just sat looking straight in front of him at some yellow flowers on a bush. He said, "What is it?" and carried on looking at the flowers. I suppose it was with Donald being a stranger – I just told him. I'd never told anybody about anything personal like that before.'

'Donald's like that,' said Tim. 'Something makes you want to trust him.'

'Now and then I've wondered if he came to sit with me because he thought he could get me to – you know – but he's never tried anything like that,' Nalin said. 'We were still talking when Angela arrived. We talked a bit more and he told her she needed to sort me out. Then he suggested going to his flat across the road. I don't know why we agreed to go home with a stranger. It's not the way either of us was brought up to behave. Well, no, I do know why – coming from him, there was nothing threatening about it.'

People were beginning to return to their seats, ready for the second act.

Nalin dropped his voice almost to a whisper. 'So that was how it started. Me and Angela have been going to Donald's ever since. He lets us use it as our "love nest", as he puts it.'

'Did you say your brother's in Manchester doing chemistry?' Tim asked.

'First year.'

As the lights went down, Tim just had time to say, 'So is one of my school friends. I bet they know each other. I'm seeing him at Christmas. What did you say your brother's called?'

'George.'

31

Simon returned to Manchester after Christmas, anxious to know how he had done in the exams. His expectations were not good, but he wanted to believe that his pessimism was unfounded, never having done badly in exams before. Results were posted on a noticeboard halfway down a corridor in the chemistry department and he walked along with a couple of students with whom he sometimes exchanged pleasantries. He appeared near the bottom of every list and he had failed the physical chemistry paper. The other two students barely concealed their amusement, and it did not occur to him that it might be because they were relieved they were not the ones at the bottom of the list rather than out of malice.

His dismal performance would not affect his chances of getting a good degree: these exams were only intended to keep the students on their toes and provide them with something to judge their progress by. When his tutor tried to give him friendly advice on more effective learning routines, Simon dared not explain how weighed down he was with personal worries. He had read that there was a trend towards treating homosexuality as a mental illness, which could be cured by means of aversion therapy, instead of as an anti-social vice.

Undergoing treatment might end the torment of being an outcast – Simon felt utterly alone, even in the midst of friends – but it was unwise for anybody to express doubts about their sexuality to anyone in authority. A rumour had gone round about two men who had been sent down from university after they took a shower together in one of the halls of residence.

His growing friendship with George gave him something to cling to through the long winter term. They went out walking and climbing every weekend, cold though the weather was, returning to the city to share fish and chips which they bought on the way back, but Simon never made any physical approach towards George. He had no idea what George's culture had to say about homosexuality, but he assumed it was negative and harsh. George might be so outraged as to tell other students, or to complain to the authorities. Even with his closest friends, the dominating influences in Simon's life were shame and fear.

They came home one evening from a day out in Derbyshire to George's ninth-floor student flat at Owen's Park. They had been walking in Lathkill Dale, and Simon had longed to hold hands with George, the way he and Cathy had done. He had remembered her touch after he'd fallen in the river that time, and had imagined stroking George's side in the same way, running his fingers down his arm, the way Cathy had done, taking hold of his hand and maybe giving him a gentle kiss.

At the flat, George had to go back down to a shop across the street for milk and coffee, leaving Simon to unwrap the fish and chips. While he was waiting, Simon noticed a poster over George's bed, encouraging people to take an interest in postgraduate research in physics. 'Do Research, and Travel' it said, listing exciting projects in exotic places. It depicted a smiling young man in stone-washed jeans and an open-necked shirt, fiddling with a piece of electronic equipment. Simon wanted to believe that George had hung up the picture because, like him, he found the man attractive. But over the desk there was a picture of Marilyn Monroe, contradicting his hopes as much as the research poster encouraged them.

Maybe there would be pictures kept out of sight? Photographs, perhaps, in one of the desk or wardrobe drawers. Simon started looking into them, listening all the while for George coming back along the corridor. He found nothing of interest – just lecture notes and clean clothing. There was a drawer beside the bed that he had not tried. As he slid it open, the sound of the lift doors came from along the corridor. He started to close the drawer, but it stuck. He pulled it out again and slid it shut just as the latch on the door rattled. He sat on the bed and tried to stop himself shaking as George came into the room.

'I was thinking,' he said to George. 'Did you used to eat chips in Cambridge or was it always rice and stuff?'

'Well, rice, yes, and plenty of other things. We never had fish and chips. They're supposed to be cooked in beef fat. I don't know if it's true, but I don't particularly care. My dad'd go berserk if he thought I was eating them. I suppose a bit of me enjoys fish and chips because it's like holding two fingers up to him.'

'Why? He's your dad.'

'I can't say I like him. I used to respect him – at least, I suppose it was respect – it felt more like subservience. I've grown out of that.'

Simon was distanced from his own parents but for him it was not out of disrespect: it was his respect for them that made and kept him aloof. He felt he was letting them down by failing to mature into a normal, family man; they did not need to know this if he kept himself to himself.

'What about your mum. Don't you care about her either?'

'She lets him control everything. I don't know what she thinks but I know what my father thinks. He thinks I'm his creation. He's proud of his creation – his property. He doesn't care about me as me. I'm not an independent spirit. He just wants to rule me.'

George stopped for a moment and frowned.

'Perhaps he does rule me. Do you think he does?'

He picked up a chip, bit the end off and chewed it slowly.

'He's never been violent or anything. He's feeble. He gets what he wants by playing injured and helpless. I do what he wants for the sake of a quiet life until I can earn my own living – at least, that's what I tell myself. There's nothing between us.'

He turned his attention back to eating his chips methodically, one by one.

'It must leave you feeling lonely,' said Simon.

George shrugged. Simon's instinct was to hug him but his fear of a shocked rejection was stronger. He pulled off a piece of his fish and gave it to George.

32

Towards the middle of March, Simon decided, at last, to go on a trip with the university caving club. He was one of three new members who had missed the trip for novices during the previous term, and the leader of a group that planned to visit Sunset Hole agreed to let them tag along.

The minibus picked everyone up outside the Students' Union on the Friday evening and they drove in darkness to the Yorkshire Dales, to camp outside the Hill Inn. They stopped twice en route for swift pints of beer in roadside pubs, and got to the Hill Inn towards the end of the evening. After parking in a field where some other people were already camping, they went into the pub and hardened members of the Club settled into serious drinking, which Simon, wanting to be one of the crowd, tried to emulate.

By throwing out time, which was long after official closing time, it was also throwing up time, with several members of the group incoherent. As the group jostled at the exit, someone at the back suddenly shouted to be let through in a hurry. At the same moment, the landlord accidently knocked a couple of glasses off a table. An ill-tempered little terrier, excited by the commotion, ran out from behind the bar and bit Simon on the ankle.

The student who had been shouting to be let out got as far as Simon, rocked unsteadily, put both his hands on Simon's shoulders, and then vomited half a dozen pints of ale down the front of Simon's jeans. He muttered, 'Sorry, darling,' and passed out.

The others burst into laughter. Someone snatched a

soda-water siphon from the bar and started washing Simon down with it. Simon was promptly sick, too, to the further entertainment of everyone else. They caught him under the armpits, took up his feet and carried him to the minibus. Drunk as he was, he felt embarrassed, having a bunch of rough men pulling his clothes off and wiping him down with a towel. He had a sudden horror that he might get an erection, but it did not happen, so far as he could remember afterwards.

The next thing he did remember was finding himself lying on the floor of the minibus, in the pale dawn light, wrapped up in blankets, cold, stiff and desperate for a pee. He dragged himself out of the bus and relieved himself against the back wheel. Then he got back in and crawled under the blankets to doze uncomfortably, hoping it would be hours before it was time to get up.

It seemed that within only minutes other people were awake and moving around. Simon searched among the piles of gear for his clothes but could not find them. Then he saw his jeans hanging outside on a wing mirror, and memories started to come back to him. 'Oh God,' he groaned, trying to ignore the hammering that had started up in his head.

Somebody slapped him on the shoulder and laughed.

'Want your knickers?' he asked, pointing across the field to Simon's underpants, hanging from a nail on the wall of the pub.

Last night, Simon had felt ashamed of his naked body but now he did not care anymore. Being ragged by the other students gave him a feeling of belonging – it was so unlike the formalities of life that kept people aloof most of the time.

'Oh, you buggers!' he cried, surprised at his new willingness to swear, and he ran naked across the field to fetch his pants, hurting his feet on sharp stones embedded in the uneven ground. It was raining and the pants were wringing wet, but he put them on all the same and came laughing back to the minibus.

But the sense of camaraderie was already leaving him. He was not one of the crowd. If they discovered that he was drawn to some of them by their physical appeal, how would they react?

His jeans were not fit to wear; looking at them made his stomach turn. He rummaged around in the minibus, found the tattered clothes intended for use underground by the novices and chose some. The regular members of the group stuffed themselves with greasy, fried breakfasts, while Simon opted for tea and a small piece of dry bread, which he ate upwind to escape the smell of hot fat. Then they pulled ropes and ladders out of the minibus and set off up the hillside behind the pub, in the steady rain. Simon began to wonder why he had agreed to come on the trip. He felt ill, cold, miserable and frightened. It was a long walk to the cave entrance, but it still came too soon for him.

Reluctantly, he took his turn to enter it, in the middle of the group.

Once they were inside, Simon was surprised to find that he felt more comfortable. It was not the frightful place he had been imagining as they got ready at the campsite. He could walk upright in the sloping streamway, and soon found himself fascinated by the curves and angles of the water-worn rock. When they came to several short downward climbs, he found it was fun to climb in a waterfall – even a small one. Further on the water fell into a cleft, above which they traversed – a foot and a hand on each side of the drop – to reach a rock bridge, where the people ahead had fixed a ladder.

Cavers' ladders, with their flexible, wire sides, are hard to get used to. Simon's feet could not find the small rungs swaying below him, and if he tried to look over his shoulder to find them, the change in weight distribution made the rungs that his feet were on swing upwards so far that he hung by his arms with his feet stuck straight out in front of him. Eventually though he made it to the bottom. A few yards beyond the foot of the ladder the cavers climbed up a rocky slope, then crawled flat out until they came to the top of another drop – bigger than the first – that also needed a ladder.

Fred, the leader, warned that not far below the bottom of the ladder was a tricky, twisting descent followed by another ladder pitch and a second, contorted squeeze. 'Wait here if you're not happy about it.'

The other novices decided to stop where they were and an experienced member of the party agreed to stay with them, but Simon said he wanted to keep going. He could hardly believe that the vertical squeeze was passable when he got to it, even though the man in front of him, who was bigger than he was, wriggled down, feet-first, in less than a minute. Simon dreaded getting stuck, but it was too late to chicken out. He made a start and then found he had one arm jammed at a strange angle. He tried to push himself back up, but the battery hanging from his belt was snagged on something. He began to panic. He twisted his body enough to pull his arm out of its untoward position. Breathing heavily, he managed to wriggle down until he could feel that his feet were out of the bottom of the constriction. He still could not get his head low enough to see anything.

Someone called from below. 'Careful. There's a good-sized ledge but the pitch is not that far from the bottom of the squeeze.'

Simon was sure he was trapped. Resisting the urge to shout for help, he fought his way down. He was afraid he might fall down the pitch below, but he was more afraid that he would not have the strength to get back up the squeeze when they returned, fighting gravity as well as friction.

The landing was less hazardous than he had been imagining.

'That's the easy one,' said the man ahead of him. 'The squeeze at the bottom's tighter.'

Only Fred was still to come down, having let everyone else go first. Simon called up that he did not want to continue.

'Stay where you are,' Fred replied. 'You can start heading back up after I'm down.'

He descended with a certain amount of grunting but he did it easily. He squeezed past Simon and watched him make an anxious start on getting back up. Simon's feet were barely off the ground when he discovered his head was against a rock and his hat was stuck. Remembering he had to twist himself into a cork-screw shape, he came back down a little to try a different angle. His body would not bend backwards enough to negotiate the sharp turn. He ought to be facing the other way. The walls were too close for him to turn his shoulders. He bent his knees, came all the way back down, turned round and tried again.

This time he doubted that he had the strength left to pull himself into a standing position inside the cleft above him, let alone worm his way up it. After some scrabbling around, he got his chest into the tightest section, where it was so restricted that he could only breathe shallowly. He was at full stretch now, on his toes. Lifting his feet from the floor, he found nothing higher to push off from. He clawed at the wall above to drag himself up. He made progress, but something pulled at his helmet, tipping his head back. Whichever way he tried, he could not get it free.

He heard Fred beneath him. 'You all right?'

'I… think I'm stuck.'

There was a pause. 'You've got your battery cable hooked round a flake of rock. Come back down a bit.'

'I can't.'

'Yes, you can.'

Simon managed to drop a couple of inches. He would not have believed there was any spare room in the bottom of the squeeze, but Fred was used to working in confined spaces and he reached up to the place where the cable was caught and got it free.

'You're away. Shout Mark to belay you up the ladder. Don't climb it without.'

The leader ducked out of the danger area as Simon swung his feet and shot up like a rocket out of a bottle in his desperation to be free. Simon joined the others at the top of the ladder and they waited for the team below them to complete their trip. Once the first of them was back up, the party that had been waiting started on the journey out by themselves. When they got to the next ladder, they found that water was cascading down it, and a rising pool was forming beneath. Unsure what to do, they waited for their leader to catch up, moving back to get out of the spray and the cold wind stirred up by the waterfall.

'Christ,' Fred said on arrival. 'Let's go!'

He sent the experienced members of the team up first so that they could station themselves along the entrance passage, where the novices might need help. Simon's turn to climb the ladder was the last one before Fred's. The force of the water and its numbing coldness felt like an act of violence. By the time he was two-thirds of the way up the ladder, Simon was gasping for breath and half-drowned – struggling to maintain his grip on the rungs and on consciousness. The man who was belaying him pulled harder but the lifeline, tied round Simon with a bowline knot, restricted his breathing and did little to help. Fred egged him on and somehow he made it to the ledge at the top of the ladder, above the streamway.

The others moved on, leaving Simon to belay Fred who was coming up last – in their haste, no one had thought to ask whether he knew how. Simon would have known from his climbing experience but Fred did not wait to find that out. The flow of water was increasing by the minute. He free-climbed the ladder. Simon pulled up and packed the rope while Fred rolled up the ladder.

They straddled the traverse over a raging stream, where an hour before there had been a harmless trickle, and fought their way up the passage, knee-deep in foaming water. At the last climb, some of the party were still waiting. They could not withstand the force of the water coming down it unaided.

Even Fred had to be dragged up, after helping to push the others forward. A few fraught minutes later, they emerged into daylight and gathered together in the pouring rain.

Simon stood for a moment or two, then swayed, staggered aside, leaned over and started to vomit.

'Oh God,' said somebody. 'Is he still bringing last night's beer up?'

'Help him down to the pub, you two,' Fred said, recognising the signs of hypothermia. 'Shelter him from the wind. Carry him if necessary.'

They took Simon into a back room in the pub, stripped him and dried him down with a towel for the second time in twenty-four hours – this time with graver faces. They wrapped him in masses of soft, dry clothes. Slowly he began to feel brighter. After a few hours he was drinking warm tea, and ready to eat something. Later, he went to bed early in the bus, leaving the others to carouse.

By the time they set off home to Manchester the next day, he was recovered physically. He tried to make light of the adventure but he knew the others could see it had shaken him. When he joined the caving club he had aspired to become an integrated member of a team of comrades in adventure. Instead he was a feeble misfit with a shameful secret.

33

A chain of vehicles crept along the main road towards Burton-on-Trent. At its head a Morris Minor Traveller made its contented, slow progress with Arthur Hollingworth at the wheel. Mary sat beside him clutching a bottle of milk: she had not shaken off the habit of contributing something on family visits when rationing had been at its most severe. Ruth was sitting behind. They were on their way to see Arthur's older brother and sister-in-law.

'Your Aunt Hannah's been with them nearly a year now, Arthur,' Mary said. 'Oh, do pay attention.' Arthur had allowed the car to drift just as a lorry was pulling past them during a rare opportunity to overtake, but her tone of voice was one of resignation rather than alarm.

She returned to what she was saying about the family. 'It was only going to be for a week or two while she got over her fall. I can't see she'll ever be up to looking after herself again – not at her age.'

'I don't suppose she will. We all come to it in the end.'

'Linda's not in good health, you know,' Mary said. Linda was Arthur's sister-in-law. 'It must be a struggle for her. That'll be what they want to talk about. They'll have it in mind to send Hannah into a home. The cost wouldn't be a problem. She must have a fair bit put by.'

'We can't let them do that. Not after the years she sacrificed looking after Uncle Ted with his war injuries. Shut away in a home when she ought to be with the family.'

'I've been thinking the same.' Mary paused while Arthur negotiated a piece of broken brick lying in the carriageway.

The rear wheel of the car clipped it and sent it flying onto the verge. 'She could come and stay with us. If you moved your railway things into our room, we could turn the hobbies room back into a bedroom for her. Even if it wasn't permanent, it would be better than letting her go into a home before she absolutely has to.'

'I've always been especially fond of Aunt Hannah,' Arthur said. 'I had thought about the idea myself. Are you sure it wouldn't be too much of a burden? I don't want you to feel under an obligation to my side of the family.'

Ruth could not hear the conversation properly, sitting in the back seat, but she got the gist of it. She leaned forward.

'Would it help if…'

She sat back for a few seconds and then leaned forward again.

'I could move out. I'm sure Melanie would let me share Lena's house with her. I don't need to be still living at home at my age, much as I like it. Aunty could have my room.'

They had got as far as Burton and the smell from the malting floors drifted into the car. They stopped to allow a lorry to pull out of a brewery yard.

'There used to be little trains going this way and that across the road all over the place,' Arthur said, as he always did when they came here. 'The tracks are still there but hardly any of them are used now.'

Mary turned towards Ruth for a moment and then faced forward again to sit more comfortably, just tilting her head back a little. 'We have noticed what a lot of time you spend with Melanie, haven't we, Arthur?'

Arthur smiled and said, 'Mmm.' As the lorry moved out of the way and they set off again, he added, 'We're pleased for you.'

Ruth looked out of the side window, still listening to what she could hear of the conversation.

'Do you think it would be all right with Lena?' Mary asked.

Ruth waited a moment and then added, 'She's already suggested I can, if I want to.'

'I'm not so sure about Harold,' Arthur said. 'What's he going to make of it?'

'Harold, bless him,' Mary replied, without waiting for Ruth to speak. 'He's such an innocent old thing. I'm sure he'll just see Ruth as a nice companion for Melanie.'

'Now you put it like that, I suppose that's what she is in the end,' Arthur said.

'He knows I go around with Melanie a lot,' Ruth said. 'He seems to be happy with it.'

'All the same,' Arthur said, 'moving in would be a bit different.'

'Harold's heart's in the right place,' Mary said, as they pulled up outside Arthur's brother's house. 'You'll see.'

34

When Simon received a letter from Tim suggesting that they and George go to a weekend climbing event in North Wales early in May, organised jointly by the Manchester and Cambridge University Climbing Clubs, he took no action for a week or two, intending to reply that it was too late to get places. Tim had confirmed at Christmas that Nalin's brother and the George who Simon climbed with were the same person. He was keen to be introduced. But Simon had not forgotten his unhappy caving trip. He had little confidence in his physical abilities now, and none in his ability to cope in a crowd dominated by the masculine spirit.

He and Tim had grown up together and, in that time, hardly ever been separated, but when they began their university studies, they had both been ready to move on. Now Simon regarded Tim as an old friend and not a lover… perhaps not even an ex-lover. Had they been lovers? Their romance had grown out of their childhood attachment. They had always been together, and he hoped they would always be special friends, but in their restricted village life Simon had not understood the multifarious gradations of friendship and love.

He remembered wondering whether Tim was in love with him or just enjoying the sex. It was not important anymore. It was when they were together at Christmas that the metamorphosis from schoolboy chums experimenting together to mature friends had taken place. The change had been a reluctant acceptance of reality for Simon, rather than a choice, but even if they had been lovers, they were lovers no longer. If George sensed there had been something more than 'naturally' intimate between Simon and Tim, he might turn against Simon.

The delaying tactic failed because George saw the trip listed in the club programme. 'Why don't we go on this weekend in Wales? You could ask that school friend to come that's in Cambridge.'

There was no way out.

'Tim's already written to me about it,' Simon admitted.

George and Simon could not travel in the club minibus from Manchester as it was leaving mid-afternoon when they would still be working in the laboratory – what easy lives the students doing other subjects got. They went on the evening train instead, planning to walk and hitch their way from the station.

They were lucky, and got a lift with a local farmer to within a couple of miles of the climbing hut, but it was still very late when they arrived. All the lights were out except one, just inside the door, left on for their benefit, and the other members of both clubs were asleep in the dormitory. George and Simon went straight to bed, too. Simon had never stayed in a club hut before and did not know what to expect. He was astonished by the one huge bed in the dormitory bearing a heap of softly breathing people.

'Where do we go?' he whispered to George.

'Burrow yourself a space.'

George crawled onto the bed and wriggled into a promising gap between two sleepers. Simon did the same, squeezing between two men who half-woke, grumbled and moved just enough for him to get in. In different circumstances he would have found the situation too arousing to cope with but, tired as he was, he only felt warm and secure, and he was soon asleep.

In the morning the sun was shining and the air was

pleasantly cool, but much time was lost over a leisurely breakfast and lengthy discussions about choices for the day. Tim had been on a few trips with the Cambridge club and he had been pushing his grades. He was keen to try for a challenging classic, such as Cemetery Gates on Dinas Cromlech in Llanberis Pass. Simon was alarmed by the suggestion. He looked at George for support and George said the proposal was over-ambitious. It would be wiser to do some more straightforward climbs – Flying Buttress and Spiral Stairs maybe.

'They're supposed to be absolute classics and they're only rated "diff".'

Someone who had overheard them said he wanted to climb Cemetery Gates and asked Tim if he would be his second.

'Isn't the crux near the top of the first pitch?' Tim asked. 'If you do that, I think I could lead the second one but I'd be happier if you led both. I'm sure I'll get up it if I second.' He turned to George and Simon. 'Is that all right?'

'We'll be fine,' said George.

The minibus dropped them off at Dinas Cromlech at eleven o'clock, before taking some of the others to spend the day on Tryfan. Even the steep slope from the roadside to the foot of the climb made Simon feel uncomfortable. Once they had put on their harnesses, he got ready to belay George and stood looking up at the spire of rock they were about to ascend.

'No, you're leading,' George said.

'I'd rather second.'

'I know you would, but you'll like leading this.'

He started transferring gear from his own belt to Simon's. The clicks of the karabiners and the pull of their weight at Simon's waist made him feel like a climber instead of merely Simon.

'I'll watch you,' said George.

It is a phrase that means everything to a climber. When it comes from a trusted partner – the promise to watch over, and not simply to observe – it inspires confidence beyond its immediate import.

'I'll give it a go.'

'Climb when you're ready.'

'Climbing.'

The first few holds were polished but they were big and Simon was able to put in protection when he was only a few feet off the ground.

'Got you on pink,' came the calm comment from George.

Simon moved on, discovering that his nervousness was evaporating. When he reached the pinnacle of the buttress, it delighted him. He stood atop it, with long, sheer drops on three sides and a steep climb down the fourth to a thin wall of rock leading to the main cliff face. He was not afraid – only exhilarated by being in such a place. He made himself safe and belayed George.

'Are you leading through?' he asked when George arrived. 'No, you carry on. Traverse left across the cliff face.' Simon looked at the drop. 'Wow!'

The handholds were exactly where they needed to be and there were excellent placements for protection. A pair of strangers were climbing the next pitch, and the seconder was belaying, tucked against the cliff behind a flake of rock. As Simon approached, the stranger glanced towards him and then, turning his attention back to watching his leader at the top of the pitch, he said, 'Shan't be long. Move onto the outside of the flake – there are some good holds.'

Simon did as the stranger suggested. What a place to be waiting in a queue. He stood with his fingers curled round the rock flake which came up to about chest height. As the stranger had said, the footholds and handholds were secure, and Simon would be unlikely to fall off. Even if he did, the rope would save him. The drop beneath his feet led right down to a grey-green slope at the foot of the cliff, but again Simon was exhilarated rather than frightened.

The lead climber ahead, on rock that looked warm and inviting, was silhouetted against a pure-blue sky, arranging a belay so that his second could follow him. The second was dressed in scarlet and the brightness of his clothes set off the blackness of his hair, which curled appealingly over the rolled-up hood of his jacket. He moved on, and Simon took over the comfortable stance behind the flake to belay George across the cliff face.

Once George had made himself safe, Simon climbed straight up and onto a sloping ledge. There were only thin cracks here in which to place protection, but Simon was happy with what he found, and he kept going. At the top of the climb he arranged a belay and sat with his feet dangling over the edge to bring George up. He was aware of how nonchalantly he did this and knew that his self-confidence was returning. Seated where he was put him in mind of the time he had watched Chris perched the same way to belay Nicola on the climb at Thor's Cave. He imagined what he must look like, with his flame-coloured hair aglow in the light from the sun behind him, and hoped that George would notice.

They found a safe descent and walked to the start of Spiral Stairs, which George would lead. It was at the other end of the crag, close to the climb chosen by Tim and his partner for the day, but they had already disappeared from view.

A good climber moves with the grace of a ballet dancer, even on a simple climb, and Simon watched George, admiring his methodical style and elegant movements. Though the men were apart on the cliff, the rope, and the function it performed, held them in communion. George – in his green shirt and darker-green shorts, which were crumpled into a loose bundle high up his thighs from the pull of the harness – was tantalisingly attractive. A loveable youth, with his clothes in disarray, and a strong man brimming with sexuality all in one. Simon wanted him desperately and it made him feel ashamed: not ashamed of his nature but ashamed to treat George so disrespectfully, as an object to be desired.

The minibus returned in the last light of the day to take them back to the hut. Climbers are a different breed from cavers. They had a few bottles of beer and some wine, but there was no drunken party. It was a relaxing evening, passed with conversation about the climbs of the day and hopes for more on the morrow. Simon enjoyed being in bed with a dozen other people and fell asleep with his head laid against another man's shoulder. He was not sleeping next to George, and he was glad of that: he would have found it hard to prevent his hands from wandering to George's body. He was not sleeping next to Tim, either. It was George who found himself snuggled up against Tim.

They woke to pouring rain. A couple of enthusiasts insisted on going climbing in spite of the weather, but most of the others preferred to stay in the hut and discuss plans for future trips. George suggested that Simon, Tim and he should go for a walk in the rain.

'What do you expect in Wales? It's better than sitting in a room full of cigarette smoke.'

They undertook to be back at the hut by 4 pm, and set off on a walk that would take them into Capel Curig by midday, where they could visit a café. It was an extravagant alternative to taking a packed lunch for three students on tight budgets, but one they decided to allow themselves. Popular belief has it that there is something especially wet about Welsh rain. By the time they reached Capel Curig all three of them were glad they had opted to get lunch somewhere warm. The moisture rising from their sodden clothes combined with that coming from the other occupants of the crowded café, and condensation streamed down the windows, pools of water forming on the floor. The Formica table tops glistened. The three men squeezed through the crowd of customers to the only vacant table, at the far end and close to the serving counter, where the warmth and humidity made it feel like being in a hot shower.

A damp newspaper had been abandoned on the table and Tim picked it up to make room for their mugs of tea and plates of eggs and chips. The headline, PROFUMO AFFAIR STILL MATTERS, caught his attention, and he read a couple of lines beneath it before tucking the newspaper behind the tray Simon had propped against the wall, for want of anywhere else to put it. He turned to the other two.

'That was years ago. Half the conservatives getting mixed up with a prostitute. I can't see why it's getting dragged up again.'

'One or two of them – not half of them,' said George. 'Assuming it was true.' He paused. 'At least Profumo fell naturally. Not like Vassall – that queer who got sent to prison. It must have been a bit before Profumo got into the news. You wouldn't think I was old enough to understand. It's surprising what you pick up on even at that age. He wasn't just a spy. He was a pervert as well. He'd got a man for a lover.'

Tim opened his mouth to comment, but something about the look on Simon's face stopped him.

35

A damp, winter evening in Cambridge, halfway through Tim's second year at university. He had spent two hours hovering around the toilets at Four Lamps without finding anyone. Cold and tired, he walked despondently along Sidney Street, half thinking he might go along to the Stable Bar. He changed his mind. When he turned onto Petty Cury en route to the college, he became aware that a group of young men was following him. As he crossed the dark Market Square, the group caught up and surrounded him.

'Fucking queer,' grunted one of them, pushing him in the chest. Another, behind him, thumped him with two fists under the kidneys. The one in front swung something hard and heavy into Tim's face. The group punched and kicked him, and he fell to the ground and curled into a ball in an attempt to defend himself. All the time, they shouted abuse.

The attack was short and vicious. After less than a minute the assailants had gone, leaving Tim slumped beside the refuse skips in the midst of the market stalls. He lay still for a while, then sat up and felt inside his mouth with his fingers to pull out a piece of broken tooth and explore the stump protruding from his aching gums. His head was covered in bruises and his body shook.

He got up and began to stagger, not towards Gonville and Caius College, but towards Donald's flat on Trumpington Street. A few couples sauntered arm in arm through St Mary's Passage on their way from the theatre as he went the other way. They glanced at him but noticed nothing, because he walked in the shadows. He did not want the attention of strangers; he wanted to creep away secretly, like a wounded animal going to its lair. He only wanted Donald.

As he walked in front of the Fitzwilliam Museum, he stumbled sideways, and fell into the culvert that some benefactor had long before decreed should flow in perpetuity for the good of passing horses. Even as he tripped, he was anticipating the impact of the hard-edged stone, and when it came, he felt a sharp pain in his left arm. There was no one to see his fall, and he was glad of that.

He limped to Donald's flat. Seeing that there were no lights on, he took out his key and went in, leaving the door open while he felt his way along the hall to find the light switch. His foot struck something big and soft and he did not need to see it clearly to realise what it was. He reached over and put the light on to reveal Donald's slumped body. A wine glass lay on the floor and red wine had been splashed onto the wall. There were no obvious signs of injury. He knelt down beside him, shook his shoulder and repeated his name, willing him to open his eyes, but there was no response. Tim stood up again. He had been reluctant to seek medical help for himself because the reason for his assault might come out. Now he picked up the telephone and asked for an ambulance, before collapsing over the table where the telephone stood.

Discovering a battered young man and the dead body of an older man, the ambulance crew gave priority to Tim. They carried him out on a stretcher and were still loading it into the vehicle when a police car arrived. A policeman came over and spoke to Tim.

'Somebody will come to talk to you later.'

The ambulance took Tim to Addenbrooke's Hospital, leaving the police in charge of the premises, where they began a search. Later, they took away, among other things, a torn pair of jeans that they found in the bottom of a wardrobe.

An examination at the hospital established that Tim had lost part of a tooth, which he already knew, might have a cracked bone in his arm, which he had already guessed, was badly bruised, but had no broken bones. He did not appear to have dangerous internal injuries, but they kept him in as a precaution, explaining that he would be able to go home towards the end of the next day. When he woke the following morning, a detective was waiting to speak to him.

'I gather they found you knocked about and sprawled across a table.'

Tim's memories were confused, but he recounted most of what had happened. He said nothing about what he had been doing before he was attacked in the Market Square, and he gave no reason for choosing to go to Donald's house. The police were always on the lookout for homosexuals and getting yourself beaten up could be a pretty sure giveaway.

'You weren't attacked in the flat?' Tim gave just the slightest shake of the head. 'Have you any idea why anyone would want to follow you into the Market Square and beat you up?'

Tim shook his head again.

'The Market Square can be a rough place at night but there is usually something…'

It was obvious what this questioning was about. The detective gave him a card with a phone number on it.

'Call if you decide there's anything else you ought to have told me.'

If the detective accepted the truth that Tim had been beaten up in the Market Square, it would not take much imagination to work out why. If he had got the idea into his head that Tim had been beaten up in the flat, the obvious question would be how he came to be there. Until now, the rumours that circulated about Donald Wolfcote had been quietly ignored: this was the usual practice on coming across any hint of a university staff member's penchant for young men.

‘The flat we found you in… According to the nurse, your address is Gonville and Caius.’

‘I just went to the nearest house I saw when I couldn’t keep going.’

‘How did you get in?’

Tim pictured Donald lying in the hallway unable to answer the door and guessed that Detective Inspector Latham was doing the same. He said the only thing he could think of: ‘The door wasn’t properly shut.’

There was just a hint of a smile on Inspector Latham’s face. ‘Let’s leave it at that.’

36

The evening he returned from hospital, Tim busied himself with inconsequential things, flitting about the room and moving books and papers back and forth with shaking hands. The police were sure to suspect he was a regular visitor to Donald's flat and broaden their enquiries. They would be taking an interest in where else he went, and why. He could not get fearful thoughts out of his head. If they found out he was a 'practising homosexual', as they liked to call it, he could land in prison for as long as an assault conviction would get him, maybe even longer. He certainly wouldn't be treated as a victim of assault. From the stories he had heard, it did not matter whether the police found clear evidence. Tim believed that mere suspicion would be enough for them to give him a hard time.

He was about to get into bed when there was a soft tapping on his door.

He assumed it was the police, coming to question him again. Had he not been preoccupied by anxiety, he would have realised policemen were more likely to arrive in the early morning than late at night. But it struck him that they would beat on the door rather than play on it with soft fingertips. Perhaps a fellow student had taken a fancy to him and wanted to be admitted without anyone else noticing.

When he opened the door and found Nalin standing there, Tim looked at him blankly for a moment. Noticing that Nalin looked unkempt, his clothes dusty, Tim's expression changed to one of concern. 'What's wrong?'

Nalin came in. He was carrying a small backpack. He

walked across the room and sat on the edge of the bed, clutching the bag in his arms and resting his bearded chin on the top of it. Tim closed the door.

'My dad's thrown me out,' Nalin said.

'Why?'

'Yesterday. He threw me out.'

'He can't have. He'll change his mind.'

'He won't. I know him.'

'Oh, now I get it.' Tim smiled and sat down next to Nalin. 'You've told him about Angela at last. He had to find out some time.'

Nalin half shook his head, put his bag on the floor and turned to look forlornly into Tim's face. 'He hasn't found out about Angela.' When he continued, his voice was tight and controlled, like somebody in shock who is trying to make nothing of it. 'He's found out about Donald.'

'You mean about you going there, or him being...?'

'Dad wouldn't care what some university professor did with his students. He'd be delighted to gossip with his friends about it. He'd put it down to the loose morals of the English. It's one of his favourite subjects. But he's found out I've been going to Donald's flat and that's different. He thinks he can put two and two together...'

Nalin noticed the bruises on Tim's face for the first time.

'What's happened to your face?'

'Oh, nothing. I got into a bit of a fight in the Market Square.'

Nalin paused, staring at the door. 'He wanted to know how long I'd been interested in men, as he put it. He went berserk. Seriously!' He leaned forward and put his backpack between his feet on the floor. 'It was scary. I mean, it was like he'd gone wrong in the head. I thought he might go out and kill somebody. He didn't know whether to blame the English for turning me into a pervert, or blame me for letting them do it.'

Tim could not suppress a snort of disbelief. 'Your dad thinks you're a queer!?'

'I've never seen him like it before. I've told you what he's like normally – pleading and whining. Everybody knows that underneath he's just useless. He wasn't pleading this time – he was shouting. In the end he told me he was going into the shop and he wanted me out of the house when he came back. I wouldn't stay anyway.'

'Why didn't you tell him about Angela if he's got it into his head you're queer?'

'There's no point. There wouldn't be even if… He's made his mind up I'm a poof. I might as well be disowned for that as for being normal.' He glanced awkwardly at Tim. 'Sorry, I'm not saying…'

'I know. Anyway, I'm not normal according to most people. I like not being normal. Why don't you get a flat with Angela? It's time you were done with her parents as well as yours.'

'It isn't that simple.'

'Where *are* you going to go?'

'I went to Donald's yesterday but he wasn't in.'

Tim flinched. Nalin noticed but assumed Tim had felt a twinge from his injuries.

'So I hung about till later and tried again. When I got there, there was a police car outside. I could guess what that meant. I came here but you weren't in either. I spent the night in the railway station. He's been arrested. He must have been.'

They sat in silence for several minutes, during which Tim drew breath a few times as though about to speak but instead he just rubbed his eyes. Then he said. 'There's something I've got to tell you.' He scratched at an imaginary blemish on one finger of his left hand with his right thumb nail and then, still looking steadily at his hands, he said, 'Donald died last night. I went to the hospital.' It was true: he had been at the hospital, even if it was not to visit Donald as his words implied.

Nalin said, 'Was it a heart attack?'

Faced with such an immediate and direct question, Tim could not keep up the pretence.

He looked at Nalin and said, 'I went to Donald's last night. It must have been before you did. He didn't die in hospital. I found him.' He turned his eyes away for a moment before looking bleakly at Nalin again. 'I don't know what was wrong. They haven't told me.'

Nalin stood up at once and almost shouted, 'Oh God. My dad.' His eyes scanned rapidly from place to place before he turned his unblinking, wide-eyed attention back towards Tim and continued, very quietly, seeming almost to shrink into himself, 'He was so angry… He thought I was… you know… with Donald! What if…?'

'You'd better stay here,' said Tim. 'You'll have to stay tonight, anyway. You can't sleep in the street. We're not supposed to have guests for more than a night or two but as long as we're careful the porters won't notice for ages. If they do, they usually turn a blind eye. Don't jump to conclusions about your dad. It didn't look to me as though anybody had done anything to Donald.'

The college operated a policy on guests that was intended to prevent people getting lodgings without paying for them. Female guests were not allowed to stay overnight in male students' rooms at all. Any one male guest was not allowed to stay for more than three consecutive nights or for five nights total in any term. The rules were sensible enough in their way, though accidentally biased in favour of homosexual promiscuity.

Nalin hesitated.

'Don't look like that,' said Tim. 'I'm not trying to get you into bed. The whole point about sex is giving the other guy what he wants, and I know it's not what you want. Pity… You're good-looking. But you're my mate, that's all. You've got a floor to sleep on for as long as you want. And that means at least until you get yourself sorted out.'

He created a space on the floor, threw down a pillow from his bed and his sleeping bag from the wardrobe, and dropped the catch on the door lock. Nalin took a tooth brush out of his pack, went over to the wash basin and started cleaning his teeth.

37

When the results from the police forensic laboratory were delivered to Inspector Latham late one morning, more than a week after the original incident, they reported a black pubic hair trapped in the zip of the torn jeans that had come from Donald's flat and traces of a white powder embedded in the fabric. At first the laboratory had been disappointed to discover that it was neither cocaine nor heroine, then intrigued to find it was not so mundane as talc or blackboard chalk. It was magnesium carbonate, and they explained that it was the sort of chalk used by weight-trainers and gymnasts.

A lot went on behind the closed doors of university staff that was judiciously left unscrutinised by officers of the law. What was surmised to go on behind Donald Wolfcote's door was a regular topic of innuendo at the police station. From the size of the jeans, the dark-haired man who left them lying about in Wolfcote's bedroom was of small build for a weight trainer, but the chalk did not necessarily come from the wearer. He might have been in intimate contact with one. According to the experts, the narcissism of weight-trainers, obsessed with their own body image and their sense of male superiority, or their fear of its absence, could spill over into an unhealthy interest in other men.

Latham went to the swimming pool next door to the Kelsey-Kerridge gym a couple of times a week. He looked into the weight-training room the next time he was there. Every individual seemed at one moment to fit the stereotypical image of what he called a nancy boy and, at the next, to look aggressively macho.

Along the corridor, a group of people were taking part in a keep-fit class in a much larger room. The instructor was standing forward from a climbing wall on one of the longer sides of the room. A few men and women were clambering about on it. A lightly built young man appeared to have finished climbing and ready to leave. He turned to nod goodbye to someone still on the wall, presenting his back to Latham. Hanging from his belt was a little bag that was dusty with white powder and Latham saw that the man's hands were white with it.

'I was just watching the climbing,' Latham said to the man as he came out of the room.

The man noticed Latham's enquiring look at his hands.

'Chalk,' he said. 'It keeps your hands dry, to get a better grip. There was an article by a climber from America who says they are experimenting with it. So we're giving it a try.'

A brief visit to slim, black-haired Tim Gregson at Gonville and Cauis College might be informative, Latham decided.

'Have you thought of anything else I ought to know about?' asked Inspector Latham.

'Not really.'

'How's the arm?' Latham nodded towards a colourful rope stored on top of the wardrobe. 'Soon be climbing again, I hope.'

He wished Tim well and walked out down the stone stairs.

Two days later, hardly after breakfast, he was at Gonville and Caius College again. Nalin was still in Tim's room and when they heard the knock on the door, they feared it would be a porter who had noticed that Nalin was leaving the grounds suspiciously early each morning. It *was* a porter, but he had come only to bring Inspector Latham up to the room. Nalin stayed out of sight from the door but when the porter left

Tim was forced to invite the detective in.

Latham, once inside, saw Nalin and spoke to him. 'I need a word in private with Mr Gregson, if that's all right.'

'I was just going. I only came in for a minute.'

Nalin scanned the room to reassure himself there was nothing to give away that he was in residence. His bag was hidden under the bed and his clothes were inside it. The sleeping bag was under there as well – how fortunate the inspector had not arrived five minutes earlier when it was still laid out on the floor.

Nalin really had been about to go and was wearing his shoes and a lightweight coat. He nodded to the detective, said goodbye to Tim and left. Inspector Latham looked round the room. There was an envelope lying on the desk that had gone unnoticed by Nalin. Tim knew it was there and tried to ignore it, but he saw the inspector glance at the name and address.

'I've come to take you to the police station to assist with our enquiries. I need a formal statement and you can answer a few questions.'

'I've got a lecture at ten o'clock.'

'We'll be back in time for that.'

Tim picked up his coat and the two of them went out and down the stone stairs and across the quadrangle. Tim was almost paralysed with fear. He walked mechanically, trying to keep himself together. He sensed eyes watching him as he was escorted past the porter's lodge. He was put into the back of a police car waiting in the street outside and then it was a short ride to the police station on Parkside. Inside the police station, Inspector Latham reported to the reception desk and took Tim into a small, gloomy interview room. Even though the building did not seem particularly old, the furnishings and carpet looked tired and the room smelt of socks worn for too long.

'The statement should be your version of events in your own words, but it's best to keep it simple. I'll record what you tell me and you can check it and sign it.'

Tim described how he had been walking into the Market Square on his way home, when he became aware of a group of young men coming up behind him. He told Latham how they had attacked him as he crossed the Square and left him lying on the ground.

'What did they look like?' asked Latham.

'It was dark.'

'I can't believe you never noticed anything about them.'

'It was dark.'

'How many of them were there?'

'Four. No, it might only have been three.'

There was a pause while Latham composed a few sentences and wrote them onto the statement form.

'Were they tall? Short? Fat? Thin?'

'Big. I think they were big. Then they ran off but I wasn't sure they'd gone… I thought they might be waiting if I got up.'

Tim hit on an embellishment to his story that should stop Latham probing into why he had not gone back to his college for help. 'They'd seen which way I was going, so when I got up I went the other way, past the theatre. I thought I could walk to Addenbrooke's hospital.'

'Why didn't you go the nearest way, back along Petty Cury?'

Tim hesitated.

'I daren't, in case they were there.'

'You kept on walking all the way past Lensfield Road and Bateman Street?'

'Yes.'

Tim could see from the way Latham looked at him that he did not believe his story. The longer this went on, the worse it would be when they did find out he knew Donald.

Apprehensively, he said, 'I'd met Professor Wolfcote, but only a couple of times.' Latham looked hard at Tim and waited. 'Once I got onto Trumpington Street, going to his place seemed best.'

'When I saw you in hospital you said the door to the flat was open. This is a serious police investigation. If you're not being straight with me, you'll wish you had been. You're not doing yourself any favours trying to cover things up – now's the time to tell me if you were inside the flat already.'

'Do you mean when it happened?'

'When what happened?'

Tim faltered. 'I don't know.'

'Just to be clear, you were beaten up in the Market Square, not in the flat, and you weren't in the flat when "whatever it was" happened?'

'No… I wasn't there, I mean.'

'And nobody let you in.'

'No.'

'Do you want to add anything?'

'No.'

Latham finished his scribbling and handed the statement to Tim to read through. There were two spelling mistakes and it was badly punctuated. It was not the way Tim would have expressed himself, but it recorded what he had said and Latham had not written anything untoward.

Tim signed it, relieved that nothing in the written words themselves incriminated him. He was sure he was of interest to the police all the same.

'Thanks for your help,' said the inspector. 'Let's get you back to college.'

Tim was in time for his lecture but he gave it little attention. While the lecturer enthused about architectural progress during the Victorian period, his mind was going repeatedly over the horror of finding Donald in the dark hallway. It was bad enough to have found a man whose love and kindness he valued deeply lying on the floor like that. Now, by reporting it, he had got himself under investigation.

When Nalin came up to his room late in the evening, Tim sat on the bed and said, 'I shouldn't have called the ambulance to Donald's. It was obvious the police would come as well.'

'What's that got to do with anything? Of course you should have called an ambulance.'

'They're not interested in finding out who beat me up. They're only interested in why I was there and how I got into Donald's flat.'

Nalin spoke dismissively. 'I know you've got good reason to be frightened of the police but what does it matter to them now?'

Tim started to cry. 'I don't even know what Donald died of.'

Nalin sat down beside him and put a hand on his shoulder. 'Bad things happen. I loved him, you know… Not in that way… Whatever it was he died of, there wasn't anything we could do.'

'Now the police've seen you here they'll think there's something going on between you and me…'

'Did they tell you what they're investigating?'

Tim half shrugged and continued to sob. Then he turned his head towards the desk and said, 'The inspector looked at the envelope you left on there. I've put it in the drawer now but it's got your address on it – your dad's address, I mean.'

Nalin took hold of Tim's other shoulder with his free hand and turned him, so that they were facing each other. 'There's no law against being best mates.'

38

Over the years since Sigmund Freud had advised a mother that her homosexual son was neither degraded nor suffering from an illness in 1935, the psychiatric profession had moved on. A notion that held sway for a while was that homosexual men were of two kinds, described as 'inverts' and 'perverts': the inverts – women's personalities trapped in men's bodies – were easily identified by their effeminate behaviour; the perverts were men of 'normal' masculinity who found miscreant pleasure in 'unnatural' sexual acts.

By the mid-1960s, this division of types was no longer in vogue.

Homosexual behaviour was recognised as inherently deviant. Whether it was driven by depravity or some misfunctioning of the psyche, the important thing was to cure it. Treatments included electroconvulsive therapy, lobotomy, dosing men with female hormones (to supposedly dispel their interest in sex) and aversion therapy, in which a patient was subjected to electric shocks, or made to vomit through the administration of drugs, while looking at homosexual pornography.

There was contention about what caused homosexuality but, as Simon had read and told Tim when they were still living in Church Wensley, a popular explanation was that young men went through a 'vulnerable phase'. If an older man interfered with them in that state, they were easily diverted into a way of life that became permanent. It did not matter whether homosexuality was a wilful sin or an unhappy disease; either way, society needed to be protected.

Neither did it matter whether the offenders were young or old. The young needed to be reformed for their own good and so that they would not grow up into new predators, perpetuating the cycle.

The youthful, South Asian man with a beard who had been in Tim Gregson's room remarkably early in the morning might only have 'come in for a minute' as he had told Latham, but the letter on the desk to a 'Nalin Gupta' had to have been his. The address on it was not Gonville and Caius; it was either a shop or one of the houses on Mill Road. It was not far from the police station so Latham decided to walk there. Latham liked to be out on foot, rather than shut inside an office or riding in a police car.

The weather had turned cold. A bitter wind was blowing from the east but the sky was clear. A dusting of snow along the sides of the pavements, bordering a dark swathe of tarmac trodden clear by passing feet, sparkled in the winter sunshine. The address of interest was just over the railway bridge and, as he had expected, it was a shop. When he went in, the door triggered a solitary *ding* from its bell. An elderly man popped up behind the counter, where he had been bending down to get an opened carton of chocolate bars which he now placed on top.

'Can I help you?' he asked.

'I'm looking for a Mr Gupta – Nalin Gupta.'

The man behind the counter frowned. 'What have you found out about him?'

'Is he available?'

'No, he is not available. He does not live here anymore.'

'Since when?'

Old man Gupta frowned again and transferred his attention to taking chocolate bars out of the carton and arranging them in a stack at the front of the counter. It was the obvious place to tempt customers into making impulse purchases but there would have been little room for the chocolates anywhere else. The shelves were packed with cooking utensils, combs and brushes, canned food, flour, sugar, floor polish, bars of soap, soap powder, rat poison, disinfectant… The shop had the half-perfumed, half-chemical smell that goes with a household goods emporium. Bigger items like brooms and step ladders were propped in front of the shelves and there was even a row of Wellington boots, carefully graded by size.

Latham continued. 'We were called to a house where a man died recently.' Gupta stopped stacking the chocolate bars, looked briefly into Latham's eyes and then looked away. 'The man was getting on and my assumption is that he just collapsed. The matter would be of no interest to us but a student who was there and rang for an ambulance had been beaten up. When I visited him early yesterday as part of my investigation, someone who I have reason to believe was Nalin Gupta was in the college room with him.'

Mr Gupta wrinkled his nose in disgust. Then his expression changed to one more like shock. He drew in his breath sharply. 'Are you saying you think my boy beat him up?'

'Never crossed my mind. He doesn't look the type. In any case it would take more than one person to inflict the injuries the student got – and bigger men than your boy, as you call him. He seemed in a hurry to leave but it didn't look to me as though there was bad feeling between the two of them. They looked more like exceptionally close mates… if you take my meaning. I thought he might be able to throw light on a few things.'

'Mates,' echoed Gupta. He fiddled about with the stack of chocolate bars, added the last few from the carton, then took it to the far end of the shop and put it on the floor beside a couple of others. He straightened up awkwardly, rubbed his side with one hand and turned, hesitantly, to Latham.

'It's why I told him to leave. He can take what he deserves.'

'Do you want to make a formal statement?'

'He's a disgrace but he's my boy and he was led astray. I'm not going to take his side – whatever is coming to him, let it come – but I won't speak against him.'

He took a few, slow steps towards the half-open door that led to the back of the house. Latham stood and watched him. Gupta, with his hand on the door, looked over his shoulder at Latham.

'Who was it that died?'

Latham raised an eyebrow.

'It wasn't that professor on Trumpington Road…' Gupta did not finish the sentence. He lifted his right hand a little and looked at it before turning away and, after glancing again over his shoulder, pushed the door fully open and moved slowly out of the shop. Latham let him go, turned round and left the shop himself, his departure marked by the *ding* of the bell.

When he got back to the police station, the report of a post-mortem examination of Donald Wolfcote's body was waiting for him. Wolfcote had died from an intracranial haemorrhage, seemingly caused by an unlucky susceptibility to a relatively mild blow to his head, just above the left ear.

39

George was in Cambridge for the weekend only a day or two later. He would not have come home part way through term, but Nalin had told him on the telephone that he had been thrown out. He had made it sound casual but it was obvious there was something big going on. Whatever it was, it was in George's nature to show solidarity with his brother. He needed to talk face to face with him.

He stayed with his mother and father, letting them think he simply wanted a weekend at home, and arranged to meet Nalin away from the house on the Saturday. Nalin was working in the theatre for a large part of the day, but they could meet during the break between the matinée and evening performances. George suggested he ask Tim to join them a little before Nalin was due back at work. It would still leave the brothers plenty of time to talk on their own first. Nalin could get tickets for George and Tim to go to the evening performance together. Afterwards, they could pick up three takeaway meals and carry them to Tim's college room. Nalin could follow them as soon as he was free.

The café where George and Nalin met was crowded and noisy, but George realised it was better than being somewhere too quiet. No one was likely to hear their conversation and they could talk without feeling uncomfortable. A little table tucked into a corner beside the window was vacant.

'He's found out about Angela, I take it.'

'It's about me turning down that woman in Pakistan but he still doesn't know about Angela.'

'Is that what he's thrown you out for – digging your heels

in? He ought to have more sense.'

'He thinks I'm queer.'

'You!'

'Ssh. Not so loud.'

'Where's he got that from?'

Then a potential explanation occurred to George. 'Has that bloke you and Angela visit been picked up by the police?'

'Donald, you mean. I don't know how Dad found out I was going there. The only thing I can think of is, he's been following me.'

'Shack up with Angela. He'll be mortified when he realises what an idiot he's been. Giving in to what you want will be the only way out of the mess he's got himself into.'

'Things have gone too far for that.'

Nalin pushed his coffee cup to one side, leaned over the table and told George, in as soft a voice as he could in such a noisy place, about Donald's death and his suspicion that his father was responsible in some way.

'We don't know what happened. Why Donald died, I mean. Tim says he couldn't see any injuries but, well, poison wouldn't show, would it? And there must be other ways. Dad was half-crazy when I saw him. He as good as told me Donald wasn't fit to be alive. It's too much of a coincidence. I'm sure of it. Absolutely sure.'

George's face became so grave that a couple coming into the coffee bar stared at him briefly before moving on to look for somewhere to sit. He only half noticed their attention, but he glanced around the room before turning back to his brother and saying, 'You must have got it wrong. You must have.' He was shaking and his voice was uneven. After a few seconds he said, 'What are we going to do?'

Before they could discuss it, Tim came in.

Tim and George had each, separately, been to the Cambridge

Arts Theatre a few times at Nalin's instigation and enjoyed it. This would be the first time they went there together. Nalin explained that *Ross* was about a man who joined the air force and turned out to be Lawrence of Arabia. Terrence Rattigan had written the play a few years ago, but this was the first time it had been on in Cambridge. Nalin did not want to spoil their enjoyment and said nothing more except that it was considered controversial by some parts of the press. That aroused the curiosity of the other two.

Halfway through the second act the reasons for the controversy began to unfold. A Turkish general, issuing orders for Lawrence to be taken away and subjected to torture and assault, hinted at the form he wanted the assault to take, and revealed his own nature by caressing the head and neck of his subordinate. George tensed involuntarily and his knee swung sideways, causing his leg to strike Tim's and to push firmly against it for a few seconds. George was so unsettled that he was not aware of his action, but Tim noticed.

The play moved on and the brief contact ended.

As planned, they collected three Indian takeaways after the performance and went back to Tim's room. George lay on his back – across the bed, with his feet still on the floor – and closed his eyes. Tim allowed his gaze to drift back and forth along the length of George's body. Stretched out as he was, even fully clothed, it was obvious he had the lithe, muscular physique of a rock climber. Perhaps his beguiling pose was a deliberate invitation; perhaps he was so innocent that he did not even realise it was beguiling. Tim sat down beside him, resisting the temptation to fondle him, and began talking about climbing. He said he was still pushing the grades and was set on doing a couple of challenging climbs on Stanage Edge in Derbyshire when the spring came.

George replied that he seemed to have reached a plateau himself and could not get beyond it.

He opened his eyes and sat up.

'I'm not cut out to be a top-end climber. I just enjoy bumbling around.'

'You were doing great when we were in Wales,' said Tim. 'You need to get your confidence back. Why don't we do some trips to Stanage together? They're nearly all single-pitch climbs. You can belay and then second me on the ones you think look all right. You don't need to lead anything if you don't want to.'

George said he was not sure. Tim was drawn by George's lack of self-assurance and his shy manner made him even more appealing. He pressed George further, pointing out that climbing was supposed to be about the personal satisfaction of solving problems on rock faces. It did not have to involve competition.

George's eyes and deportment seemed to want to say 'yes' but his only words were, 'I don't know.'

Usually, if Tim fancied a man, he took a chance on it, but there was something about George that commanded respect. Then George looked into Tim's eyes, almost dolefully, and Tim succumbed.

He put one hand on George's knee and gently ruffled his hair with the other, saying, 'Come and share a tent with me in Derbyshire.'

George twitched his head away, and his knee.

Tim had tried it on with lots of men and been rejected at least as often as he had been accepted, but this time it really mattered to him. He was sure he had made a big mistake; he had tried too hard too soon. He wanted everything to be right between them: loving, respectful and right. He got up and reached over to the takeaways on the desk, pretending to be unperturbed and to have intended nothing. 'I can't ignore the smell of spices any longer. Let's make a start.'

They had nearly finished eating when Nalin came back. He

ignored his meal at first and dallied about taking off his jacket and putting on a multi-coloured jumper instead. When he did open up his cartons, he ate slowly and in silence, nibbling bits of chapatti as though time did not matter. George shifted about impatiently. Tim could think of nothing to say that would relieve the tension and the silence continued.

After a few minutes George got up abruptly and walked to the door. 'I've got to go. I said I wouldn't be late.'

Avoiding eye contact with Tim and looking darkly at Nalin he added, 'I'll leave you two to each other.'

He went out, closing the door quietly behind him.

40

When George returned to Manchester from his weekend in Cambridge, it was obvious to Simon that something had happened. Things were not right on the Monday morning in the laboratory, and they did not improve as the days went by. George was reserved again, even with Simon – the way he had been when they first met during Freshers' Week.

He had always been competent and meticulous. Now he was clumsy. He seemed to be distracted and let things go wrong. There was almost a disaster when he failed to notice the rapid rise of the mercury in a thermometer. It was only Simon's hasty action, pushing an ice bath under the reaction flask, that prevented a runaway eruption of vapour and boiling liquid from the top of the condenser.

It was inevitable that things got out of hand sometimes in the undergraduate teaching laboratory. Normally, the student responsible for the ill-conducted experiment released stress when the adventure was over through nervous laughter and a shaky remark intended to hide inner alarm. George appeared to be unmoved. He blinked and watched Simon regulating the experiment on his behalf, like somebody watching coffee being made in a café – waiting for the outcome but having no interest in the process.

One morning George was missing at the start of their first lecture. Simon was used to finding George already in the lecture theatre, on the front row, ahead of everybody else – driven by enthusiasm, not a sense of obligation. He crept in ten minutes late, obviously unshaven and untidily dressed. He had overslept.

It was George who spilt the sample on the bench when they were doing a radiochemistry experiment. He hardly seemed to think it mattered at first. It was obvious to Simon that George was deeply troubled, and it troubled him in turn. He stopped him on the point of using his laboratory coat sleeve to wipe up the spill, and did the job correctly for him, putting the contaminated swabs into the radioactive waste container. George became properly aware of the seriousness of what he had done and assisted. They scrubbed repeatedly until the Geiger counter ceased to click frantically when they held it close to the bench surface. He apologised and it was evident that the incident had shaken him.

Simon tried to encourage him to open up. He felt again, as he had done in Wales, the mixture of desire and the shame of looking upon George as the object of it.

'You all right?'

'Course I am. Why shouldn't I be?'

Then one day George suddenly stopped reading out measurements from a titration they were doing in the physical chemistry laboratory.

'Can I ask you something?' he said.

Simon was recording the measurements in a notebook. He put down his pen. The titration could be left for a while without coming to any harm.

'It's about when I was in Cambridge. Tim touched me. You were best mates when you were at school.'

Simon knew Tim well enough to visualise what had happened. George might report Tim to the college in Cambridge, if he hadn't done it already; he might go to the police.

'God, this is hard to talk about,' George continued. He paused. 'Nalin's living with Tim,' he said hurriedly, rushing to get his question out and stumbling over his words. 'Do you think…? Is Tim… you know… is he… are they?'

With a careless reply, Simon knew he could give himself away.

'If you want to know what I think…' he said. 'What people do is up to them. Tim would never harm anybody.'

George's penetrating stare made Simon uncomfortable. He transferred his attention to the needle of the pH meter but he sensed that George was still watching him.

'So you wouldn't disown them?' George spoke in a tone that implied he assumed Simon would.

Simon's eyes opened wide. He put his hands onto the edge of the bench. He felt the muscles of his body tense. His heart raced.

'Is that what you've done? Disowned your brother?'

George, still perched on a laboratory stool, slumped forward to rest his folded forearms on the polish-darkened, teak bench.

'Don't be shocked.'

The island bench was divided lengthways by a long, tall set of shelves, creating work spaces on both sides. Although a pair of students worked on the other side, the presence of the shelves gave Simon and George a sense of privacy, strengthened by the hum of extractor fans and the rush of water through filter pumps. If there was anyone there today, George and Simon were out of sight and their voices could not be heard. The pair who usually worked on the same side as them were not in.

George went on speaking, still resting on the bench, with his eyes directed vaguely towards the socket where the pH meter was plugged in, beneath a row of bottles filled with acrid and fishy-smelling liquids.

'My dad's kicked Nalin out of the house. I guessed why, knowing Nalin's living with Tim, but I asked him all the same. The usual way of things is, Dad comes out with what he thinks he ought to, we ignore him, and nothing changes.

He started weeping and sighing about Nalin being a filthy poofter and bringing disgrace on the family. It's what I'd expect from my Dad but it was such a big deal, I couldn't let it go.'

George had been getting more agitated as he spoke but the words that followed were controlled. 'I said he was going to have to get used to it.' He lifted his head, looked straight at Simon and, with a frown putting creases between his eyebrows and across his forehead, he blurted out, 'I told him he's got two poofs for sons.'

Simon could not believe what he had just heard. 'You mean…'

George buried his face in his hands. 'I've always known. I just didn't *want* to know. I liked it when Tim touched me. That's why I was so upset about it. It makes me ashamed, but I did.'

George lifted his head to look at Simon and asked, 'Are we still friends?'

'George,' said Simon, 'of course we are still friends.'

'I haven't told anybody else – not even Nalin.'

Simon was ready to declare his love. He opened his mouth to speak but their conversation took a different turn and the opportunity was lost, because George spoke first:

'My dad's done something bad – really bad.'

41

When George had made the revelation about his sexuality to his father, the evening he had left Tim and Nalin together during his visit to Cambridge, the old man had seemed near to despair. George could see this was not his father's usual ruse of feigning hopelessness. He sat quite still in his armchair, gazing at a faded family photograph on the mantelpiece. There was a look of desolation in his eyes as though something had snapped and left him cut adrift; as though, too late, he understood that he could not hold onto his family by imposing his will on them. He said he did not want to lose his boys.

As a little child George had clung to his father out of need. When he had started to learn to read, it was his father who sat patiently with him, pointing to the words and making him recite and spell them half a dozen times. His father was never harsh but he was insistent. If George came home from school saying he got eight out of ten in his spelling test, that was not good enough. The pressure was never-ending. It was the same for Nalin once he was old enough to go to school. There was little time for the boys to play together.

By the age of eleven, George was reading like most boys several years older. He passed the entrance examination to go to the Perse School and his father met all the costs of his education. But his father's sponsorship was not something earned. It was foisted upon him. Nalin was expected to work hard and do well at school, too, but his father did not push him into private education. It was George who was destined to fulfil his father's dreams, under a weight of privilege and unfair obligations. He never communicated to his father that his only ambition was to gain his freedom, but the tensions between them told the story with greater power than words might have done.

Old man Gupta stared at George for a long time before he said, 'I went to tell that professor Nalin's mixed up with, if he didn't leave him alone, I'd go to the police.'

'You went to his flat?' George did not divulge that he had already learned about his father's visit to Donald from Nalin.

'He seemed so harmless face to face. I said I knew what he did with young men and I wasn't having him doing it to Nalin. He wasn't frightened. He wasn't even embarrassed. He smiled. In a *kindly* sort of way, as though he was sorry for me. It was patronising. He said there were things I ought to know and I should talk to Nalin. As if I needed to!'

George's father stopped talking, as though he thought he had explained enough. Perhaps he wanted to hear George mutter something supportive, but George waited in silence, raising his face slightly in a gesture that implied, 'Go on.'

'He didn't admit anything and he didn't deny anything, either,' his father said.

George was frustrated by his father's continuing reluctance to come to the point. Why did he always play the helpless loser? Why could he not simply say what was on his mind?

'What do you mean? What did you ask him?'

'I didn't need to ask. It's obvious to me what's been happening. We didn't talk for long. He made it clear I wasn't welcome – in a polite sort of way. The English are like that. Always at their most polite when they're intentions are the opposite. He said Nalin was a grown man and I should let him make his own decisions. I'd gone there to put a stop to things – to get my way – and that man was telling *me* what to do. We couldn't have talked for more than five minutes and yet he was so clever with his words it made me wonder if he ever lost an argument. I wanted to get away.'

George watched a change come over his father's face. It was not so much to one of anger as to a memory of anger.

'When he opened the door to let me out, he was still telling me to listen to Nalin and show him respect. He said there should be love between a father and his son. He put his arm across my shoulders.' George's father grimaced and wrinkled his nose. 'I wasn't having that. I swung my arm and hit him. Not hard. I looked back at him as he stood motionless in his doorway. I wanted him to be angry but he seemed more – I don't know – disappointed. It made me feel sorry.'

George's mother came in clutching a duster but she could tell they were not going to admit her to the conversation. She wandered over to the television table and rearranged two or three ornaments and then shuffled out of the room again.

'I never meant any harm,' his father said.

George looked at his father, crumpled into his armchair. It brought back a scene from so early in his life that it felt more like watching a clip from a film than re-living a distant memory. Was he walking or crawling along the dimly lit hallway late in the evening? Surely, if he could remember it, he must have been old enough to walk. Perhaps the memory felt like crawling because he was so small. The door to the shop was open and he peeped in. His father was sitting motionless, his elbows on the counter, his hands supporting his head, staring at what must have been an open account book. Before the toddler could go through the doorway, his mother, following him, lifted him gently and took him back to the kitchen, but the expression on his father's face stayed in his mind like a phantom image on his retina. There were no tears, but small children have a way of knowing when someone is crying inside.

George had heard the story a thousand times of how his father brought the family out of their mother country at the time of the partition, when George was a baby. He had long understood how the bleakness of life in their foster country had made his father the way he was: it explained it, but it did not excuse it. Until this moment he had seen his father as an aging man, rejecting him and his brother; now he saw him as a man rejected.

He reached over and briefly touched his father's hand, where it lay limp on the arm of the chair. He could not find the words to say he cared. He went silently out of the room and up to bed.

He could not settle for a long time. More than once he thought about getting up and going to his father, but he would not have known what to say. Perhaps he did not want to say anything. He dozed and deliberated over the likely consequences of his father's actions until, without his knowing it, dreams and reality merged and he fell asleep.

His train to Manchester was mid-morning on the Sunday. His father had already gone into the shop when he got up. George would have been too confused to talk to him anyway. If he went to see Nalin, Tim would be there. So when it was time, he just put his head into the shop, said 'Bye, Dad,' and hurried to the station.

Back in his hall of residence, he telephoned Nalin. He was not able to say much, standing in a vestibule where other students passed by and knowing that Nalin would be in an equally public place. He said he had visited his father and they needed to talk about what had happened. He persuaded Nalin to come to Manchester where they would be away from the rest of the family. Nalin could not leave Cambridge immediately, but he promised to travel as soon as he could.

42

By the time Nalin arrived in Manchester, three weeks had passed since George had made the telephone call asking him to come, and it was almost a week since George's conversation in the physical chemistry laboratory with Simon. George had expected Nalin to be alone, but there was Tim, walking out of Central Station with him.

'I didn't have a chance to tell you,' Nalin said. 'We only decided this morning. Tim knows about Dad. We'll see if he can stay with Simon. It was too early to get him on the phone before we set off. If not, Tim can sleep on the floor with me, in your room.'

It was a dismal afternoon, with smoke hanging in the air and a fine drizzle drifting through the streets. The air pulsed with the heavy beat of a steam locomotive beginning its journey. The sulphurous smell of the trains mingled with appetizing smells from a Chinese restaurant and the vinegar smell of a chip shop just outside the station.

'We'd better get the bus,' said George. 'I usually walk but it takes a long time from here. Shall we get some chips before we go?'

They did as he suggested, and went to Fallowfield. Tim managed to get Simon on the telephone and Simon said he would speak to Mrs. G. and come round to Owen's Park later. The trio climbed the stairs to George's room in the tower for a spot of exercise, instead of taking the lift. George went along to the house kitchen and came back with three black coffees. 'Sorry. No milk. I didn't think to get any. No sugar, either.'

They sat awkwardly for a few minutes, knowing what they needed to talk about but reluctant to start on it – George in the one comfortable chair, the others side by side on the bed like two birds on a perch. Nalin noticed how George's gaze kept returning to Tim's handsome face, with the dark shadow of a beard that was always there even when he was freshly shaved, and to his body, snugly clad in soft-looking clothes.

'About Dad,' Nalin said. 'Have you found out for sure what he did?'

George told of how he had challenged his father for sending Nalin out of the house, but he did not mention his angry declaration about his own feelings towards men. 'You know how he does that thing of acting helpless when he wants something? He told me he had been to see the man…'

'Donald,' said Tim.

George nodded. 'He swears he just wanted to tell him to leave Nalin alone or else he'd call the police. It was when Donald put his arm across his shoulders…'

He frowned with that slight twist of the eyebrows that acknowledges the inevitable. 'It upset him. Well, you know him. He swung round and hit Donald on the side of the head. It must be the first time he's ever done anything to express himself beyond putting on his injured look.'

'One smack wouldn't be enough to kill somebody,' said Nalin. 'It couldn't be, could it?'

'Dad says Donald was fine. He hardly seemed to notice. He just saw Dad out and wished him well.'

'It can happen,' said Tim. 'You can seem to be all right and then suddenly collapse – even half an hour later. They can't blame him for something unintentional, can they? It's just one of those things.'

'It wasn't deliberate,' said Nalin. 'It wasn't murder. They can't hang him for it.'

'You don't know it was your dad's fault,' said Tim. 'I was only saying it can happen. It's probably just chance that Donald died when he did. It was going to happen anyway.'

'It's not what the police think,' George said. 'They've had Dad in for questioning. He doesn't understand properly how things work here, but from what he told me, they cautioned him. I don't see how you can call a single slap an assault, never mind murder, but you know how they are. What are we going to do?'

'It was me that found Donald,' Tim began. 'Did Nalin tell you?'

He was talking to George, but he addressed the reading lamp on the desk beside George's chair, as though he would find it a distraction to look into his eyes.

'They've questioned me twice. The second time, they got me from college. There was a letter to Nalin on my desk with your dad's address on it. That must be what put them onto him. I don't know where you got the idea they still hang people for murder, but it doesn't matter. Nothing's going to happen. They won't even get as far as taking him to court – not given the circumstances.'

'Who's going to stop them?' George asked.

Tim looked George straight in the face. It seemed to Nalin that there was a longing in the way he did it that was out of the ordinary for Tim. 'There are things I know.' He paused for a moment. 'I've seen enough of the police to know they're not interested in right and wrong – they just want to trap people any way they can and throw the law book at them. I'd do anything to help anybody up against the police and your dad's not just anybody, he's your dad… As long as we stick together.'

George looked at Tim and then at Nalin. Transferring his attention to his own, fidgeting hands, he said, 'About sticking together – I just want to say it's all right with me about you two.'

Nalin did not put him right about the mistaken implications of the remark straight away. He was not sure how much he should say. All afternoon he'd watched George and Tim. He had seen the looks between young men in Donald's house often enough to know when they were reciprocal; when they were significant. He was in no doubt about what was developing between George and Tim, but if he said the wrong thing, George might feel threatened. He wondered how long it would take them to realise their feelings were mutual.

The moment passed because George said, 'Simon should be on his way by now. Why don't we go down to meet him?'

They had only been walking for a couple of minutes when Simon came out of the thickening fog towards them. Tim introduced Nalin and Simon to each other and, as they walked back in the failing daylight, the two of them started chatting. After leading everyone up the stairs to his room, George went to make more coffee.

'Mrs G says it's all right for you to stay for a couple of nights,' Simon told Tim. 'Robin's gone off somewhere until Monday, so she says you don't need to sleep on the floor. You can have his bed.'

George came back in looking for an extra mug. Simon suggested they could go out for a Chinese meal later. The others agreed. In need of a break from the serious business of their meeting, they relaxed into a convivial evening, laughing over things they had heard on their favourite radio programmes until it was time to eat.

Conversation in the Chinese restaurant was mostly divided, between George and Tim, sitting opposite each other, and Nalin and Simon, sitting opposite each other beside them. George and Tim's connection was spontaneous. In the case of Nalin and Simon, Nalin was monopolising Simon's attention to keep George and Tim talking to each other. Afterwards, the weather was too miserable to hang around, but it was early to split up. So they decided to go back to Owen's Park for an hour or two.

They had only just entered George's room when Nalin said to his brother, 'Will the shop still be open if I go down to get milk? I don't want black coffee again.'

'You don't know where it is. I'll go in a minute.'

Nalin looked purposefully at Simon. 'Doesn't Simon know? He can take me.'

The two of them galloped down the stairs. As they crossed the courtyard in front of the student tower block, Nalin said, 'Stop a minute.'

They went into a secluded corner, not for concealment but because it felt warmer being tucked in close to the walls.

'Do you know Tim really well?'

His question was an echo of the start of George's confession to Simon in the laboratory. When he replied, he looked defensive. 'We went to school together. Why?'

Nalin noticed Simon's discomfort. Perhaps Simon feared that he was trying to probe into things that he would not want to him to know about. It reminded Nalin of how he had felt himself when his family started asking questions about his women friends.

'Sorry. There was something I wondered about but it's not important. Another time, maybe.'

They collected the milk and went back upstairs.

Coffee was soon made and drunk. Simon got up, saying, 'We'd better be going, Tim. It takes about twenty minutes.'

'Why don't I go back with Simon?' Nalin said. It'll give us the chance to get to know each other.' He angled his head towards his brother, commenting good-naturedly, 'I see more than enough of him.'

'I told Mrs G Tim was coming because he's an old school friend,' Simon began. Nalin dipped an eyebrow. 'But I don't think she'll mind.'

George looked apprehensive. Tim gave the appearance of not being bothered either way.

'Fine. That's settled,' said Nalin. 'Come on, Simon.'

As they left the room, he glanced fleetingly at Tim. Purposefully choosing his words he said, 'We'll leave you two to each other.'

43

Mrs G had already gone to bed when Simon and Nalin got back. Simon went through to the kitchen to boil the kettle, made cocoa, and brought it back in. Nalin noticed the football trophies and photographs on the sideboard.

'There are more on the window ledge behind the curtains,' Simon told him. 'It's Mrs G's son. I'm not all that interested in football. Are you?'

Nalin gave a slight shake of the head.

They talked on and off about nothing in particular, both of them aware that they were postponing a question waiting to be put and answered. Eventually they finished their cocoa and went upstairs to bed.

'This is your bed,' said Simon. 'Mine's the one by the window.'

After they had been in bed for a short time they got back into conversation. 'I think I've made a big mistake,' said Nalin.

Simon's sheets rustled as he turned over to listen. 'Why?'

'Tim made a pass at George last week in Cambridge. When we went to get the milk and I asked how well you knew him, I was going to ask if you knew he liked men. As soon as I'd started asking, I realised it would be a silly question. You must do, being friends for so long. He doesn't exactly keep it a secret. That's why I dropped the subject.'

'I guessed it might be something like that.'

'He thinks he's screwed things up with George and he's really upset. I've never seen him serious about anybody before… It's usually something more frivolous and with Donald it was only a sugar daddy thing. He's fallen in love properly at last and he goes and chooses my bottled-up brother.'

'I thought you and Tim…'

Nalin went on, too deep in thought to notice what had been said. 'George's been hiding something ever since he was about fifteen. George being George, he's never let on but it's been obvious to me what's been going on with him for long enough. When I suggested we left them together tonight, it was my attempt at match making.'

Nalin was quiet for several minutes and then he added, 'It's a disaster if I'm wrong.'

He propped himself up on one elbow.

'Tim will be devastated if George turns him down.' He lay down again, looking straight up at the ceiling.

'He's more sensitive than people think. I can tell he respects George. I wouldn't stand by and let things happen to my brother if I didn't think that. Tim's always been a bit of a predator but he doesn't want George to see him that way. I should have thought it through. If Tim makes an approach… Even if George does fancy him, he's not going to admit it. He'll think Tim should be ashamed, the way he's ashamed of himself. It's simple psychology. He *will* see him as a predator and he'll hate him for it.' He sat up and pushed his bedclothes aside. 'We ought to go back before it's too late.'

'I thought you and Tim…'

Nalin gave an unselfconscious chuckle. 'I know what he gets up to when he goes out but there isn't anything between him and me. That's what makes us friends. We'd probably have fallen out and split up long ago if we were lovers! I'm not into men. The stuff with Dad came up because I'd got a girlfriend he didn't know about.'

He explained how he and Angela used to meet in Donald's house and that it was there he had come to know Tim.

Simon wondered why Nalin and Angela did not take control of their own lives and set up home together. Nalin said, 'She's ruled by her parents.' His voice briefly took on a mocking tone. 'They don't like anything that spoils their narrow little world. Asians coming and settling in their nice clean city, for example.' Then he spoke more seriously. 'It struck me a couple of months ago that she didn't really love me. She was using me as a mechanism to hit back – a way to be defiant – to escape from them.'

Late-night conversations in the dark encourage men to share confidences.

Nalin stopped for a moment and cleared his throat. Pausing between each sentence he said, 'You see what's wrong with you in other people before you see it in yourself. I was using her the same way she was using me – I wanted to kick against Dad. I couldn't tell her in so many words. I just went cool and we've drifted apart. I haven't told George. Or Tim.'

He got out of bed.

'Come on. We've got to go back to George's.'

'We don't need to,' said Simon.

Something allowed him to go on, and he told Nalin about his conversation in the laboratory with George. Perhaps it was because they were still almost strangers; perhaps it was because, despite that, he already trusted him; perhaps it was the calming influence of talking in the dark. He needed understanding and Nalin was someone who would understand.

'I'm in love with George, too. He doesn't know.'

If only I had dared to tell George a few months ago, he thought. A powerful, unspoken fear governed Simon's life: the fear of rejection – rejection by everyone, but especially rejection by a man he loved. It had stopped him speaking and now it was too late. If the world had not been so harsh on people like him, perhaps he would have been brave enough to take the risk. George was brave and he had chosen someone else. Simon wanted George to be happy and he was strong enough at least to rejoice in that happiness.

The relief he felt, getting beyond his fear for the first time and confessing to Nalin, encouraged him to say more.

'It's hard for me, what's happening between him and Tim. I used to be Tim's lover when we were still at school. I still love him but not like that anymore – in a different way. I can see now splitting up was the right thing to do. I've got over it. In time, I'll feel the same about George. I want them to be happy – both of them.'

He waited a long time before he added, his voice tense with apprehension, 'You're the only person… other than Tim… who knows about me.'

'It can't be easy living in a footballing household with the attitudes football supporters have,' Nalin said.

'Don't tell anybody.'

Nalin got up and sat on the side of his bed that faced Simon's and the window. He looked tenderly for a few seconds at Simon's silhouette against the amber light filtering through the curtains from the streetlamp outside. He slid under his own sheets and settled down ready to sleep. 'Nothing's ever simple.'

44

Mrs G was clattering around in the kitchen when Nalin and Simon woke up the next morning. When they came down, their breakfast of eggs, bacon, black pudding, tomatoes and fried bread was keeping warm in the oven. She brought it to them in the front room, setting it down on the table close to the window. Nalin's brown face took her by surprise.

'Are you Tim?'

Simon chipped in to explain that Nalin had done a swap with Tim. He let it seem that Tim and George had wanted to stay out late but he and Nalin had been tired and ready to come home. Mrs G had her doubts about 'those darkies', but they were more conjectural than concrete. They applied to the world of unknowns, not to this smart young friend of Tim's with a handsome face. When she said Nalin was welcome, it was genuine.

She went back to what she was doing in the kitchen and turned on the radio. The distant sound of 'Mrs Brown, You've Got a Lovely Daughter' came through into the living room. Nalin, still standing, looked at his plate and raised his eyebrows.

Simon sat down at the table. He nodded towards the breakfast and said, 'I didn't think, with you coming instead of Tim… Is it all right?'

Nalin sat down, too. 'I don't worry about every last smidgeon of meat. I'll have your eggs and you can have my bacon and black pudding. I'm not sure about the fried bread.'

'Give me that as well. There's plenty of toast.'

'George eats everything. I agree with him in principle.

There's more to religion than following little rules. I only keep off pork because I don't fancy the idea.'

'Mmm.' Simon had his mouth full of food.

Mention of religion had reminded him that it was Sunday. It was nearly ten to ten. They had slept in longer than he had intended. Cathy would be arriving within the next minute or two. He looked out of the window, but the street was deserted, apart from a cat sitting on the pavement in front of the house opposite. He noticed the silver cup on the window ledge and remembered how, on the day he had first come to the house, it had reflected a distorted image of his face. He had been a stranger then. He was still a stranger. Football meant everything in this house and nothing to him, but that was not it: he did not belong anywhere. If he went closer to the cup, he would still see the same unnatural reflection in it. He turned to look at Nalin, who had picked up the Sunday paper and was preoccupied with reading. At least now there was one person who knew, and they had not rejected him: telling Nalin had made him a closer friend in fact – the one friend with whom every secret could be shared.

Mrs G came in to clear away the breakfast things. The fire she had put a match to earlier was burning nicely, so she went to the grate first, to partially shut the air vent at the front, pushing it round with her toe. As she was stacking the last of the plates onto her tray she looked out of the window.

'Here's Cathy,' she said.

'We go to church together with the Christian Union. I forgot to tell her I'm not going today,' Simon said to Nalin, as Mrs G went out of the room to open the front door, carrying the tray with her. She balanced it on one hand while she released the door catch with the other. 'They're in the front,' she said to Cathy, taking hold of the tray with both hands again, turning and going to the kitchen.

Cathy came through to the living room. She was wearing

a pale-blue coat, with a matching hat trimmed with a little bunch of false pearls on one side and a veil that was decorative rather than functional, barely reaching down to her eyebrows. In one hand she had a small, white handbag and in the other she held a brown, leather-bound prayer book.

'Hello,' she said to Simon, surprised that he was wearing jeans rather than a suit. 'Are you ready?'

She smiled enquiringly at Nalin.

'I'm just here for the weekend,' Nalin said.

Then Simon said, 'Cathy, I'm sorry. I completely forgot to tell you. I can't come to the service this morning.'

Cathy put on the appearance of mild disappointment but she was really suppressing exasperation. When was Simon going to come out with the truth? It had seemed obvious to her for a long time. This morning it was more obvious than ever.

'Oh, it doesn't matter,' she said.

'It's my fault,' Nalin said. 'Simon didn't have a chance to tell anybody.'

'Really, it's all right,' she said. She studied his open smile and the even brown of his face. 'You wouldn't have wanted to come to church with us, I don't imagine.'

'I'm not strict about being Hindu. I can't speak for my brother – but he probably doesn't want to believe in anything. My dad thinks we ought to be "true to our roots", as he puts it. I don't see why it's such a big issue to follow our own paths. There shouldn't be all this antipathy between religions, I know that much.'

'His brother's George,' said Simon. 'The George I go climbing with. Nalin's come to see him.'

Cathy was still thinking about what Nalin had just said. 'I agree. We shouldn't be divided by religion.' She looked thoughtfully at Nalin and Simon who were standing close together, almost touching hands. Almost touching, but still apart. 'Or by anything else,' she said.

Mrs G put her head round the door. 'Are you staying? I'll put the kettle on.'

'Thanks, but I ought to be going.'

Cathy picked up her prayer book. 'See you next week, Simon.'

She gave him a little kiss on the cheek. Simon did not respond. As she said a polite goodbye to Nalin, she looked him up and down quickly and her gaze lingered a little on his face.

'Perhaps you'll be in Manchester again. It'd be nice to get to know you.'

After she had gone, Nalin asked Simon, 'How do you know Cathy?'

There was a twitch at the corner of Simon's mouth and he glanced at the door as though he wanted to reassure himself Cathy had gone. 'She's my girlfriend. We're both Baptists.'

Nalin gave him a disapproving look and was about to speak, but Simon spoke first. 'She's a friend who is a girl, I mean.'

45

Tim had a strategy to get Nalin's father out of trouble, but he had not worked out how to implement it. The opportunity came unexpectedly when he was out on the River Granta. It was warm for a winter day. The air was still, and the sun shone gently onto his left side as he punted upstream from Cambridge towards Granchester, casting a long shadow that dipped and swayed across the water with the graceful movement of his body. Once he got beyond the Backs, there was no one else on the river, and he enjoyed the slow, rhythmical splash and swirl as he worked the pole up and down. There was hardly another sound, except for the twittering of a few birds.

It was much-needed relaxation, and he was thinking of nothing else until he saw two men strolling back towards Cambridge on the path through Granchester meadows: two friends out for a walk with a little dog. They were talking happily. They did not pay attention to him, but he paid attention to them. They interested him a lot. One of the men was Inspector Latham.

Tim did not know the name of the other, but he had met him at Four Lamps and he had seen him in the Stable Bar.

After the men had passed, he watched them over his shoulder. They stopped at a gate and chatted for a short time, although they were too far away for their voices to carry to Tim. Then Inspector Latham turned back towards Granchester, and hence towards Tim, while the other man went on his way with the dog. Tim steered his punt to the bank, close to an overhanging willow. He hopped onto the land, secured the punt to the tree, crossed the wet meadow and intercepted Latham.

He waved towards the punt. 'I was on the river. I've been thinking about coming to see you… I don't like police stations.'

Latham smiled. They stood side by side, watching a couple of broken twigs drifting past the punt. The river was slow-moving, and the twigs bumped together and hesitated before gliding on their way.

'Have you caught anybody?' Tim did not let on that he knew Gupta was under suspicion.

'We've got our ideas.'

'Only you said if there was anything I thought of…'

'Go on.'

'According to the *Cambridge Evening News*, Professor Wolfcote died of natural causes.'

'You don't believe everything you read in the papers, do you?'

'Do you think somebody killed him?'

'It's a possibility I'm investigating, if that's what you mean.'

Latham looked around. There was nobody on the path and nobody on the river. 'We both know what used to go on in that flat,' he said. 'It's been an open secret for years. Just as long as the university kept itself to itself I was happy to leave them to it.' He glanced back along the path again. 'I know what you'd been doing when you got beaten up. You got what you deserved. I might call that enough, but it's not my job to decide what counts as justice. There's a case to answer if I decide to pursue it. Giving me a bit of help might not do you any harm.'

'I'd better be going,' Tim said. 'I don't want to get people into trouble.'

It was a ploy to make his purpose less evident. The politicians would not thank Latham for revelations about the sexual proclivities of the people Tim was about to name. But it must not be obvious that he was out to gain the upper hand. Faced with a covert attempt to pervert the course of justice, how would Latham react? Which would win: his belief in the strict application of the law, or fealty to his seniors and the need, in his own interests, to defend their public respectability? It had to look as though Tim was only making the disclosures out of desperation, under pressure. He took a small step backwards and turned his head towards the punt.

'Out with it,' said Latham.

Tim fidgeted with the sleeve of his jacket and rolled a couple of stones around under his foot. In the secretive community Tim belonged to, respecting people's anonymity was a rule of honour. If things went the wrong way, he would not be forgiven for the betrayal he was about to commit. But it was a risk that had to be taken. He gave Latham the names of two men he had met at Donald's. They were names that would set Latham thinking: the police superintendent in a neighbouring town, recently promoted from the Cambridge force, whom he was sure to know; and the magistrate in the same place. Tim did not know if there was an illicit side to their lives or not. He only knew that they sometimes visited Donald. But Latham would make his own assumptions.

Tim could see from Latham's face that the implications of blowing their cover had hit home. He added the information he had gained only minutes before: 'And I don't know his name, but the man you were with when I saw you on the path a few minutes ago.' This man, Tim knew from intimate personal experience, was unquestionably a 'friend of Dorothy's'.

He was right to include him, though he would never have guessed how right. The man was the Worshipful Master of the Masonic Lodge to which Latham belonged.

46

On the day that Tim went on his punting trip, Nalin was in Manchester with George again. He and his brother had agreed to meet so that they could discuss what was happening to their father on their own.

'We can't turn our backs on him,' George said.

They were sitting in George's room, looking out high over Fallowfield. Viewed from nine floors up, the neighbourhood was a forest wreathed in smoke, with houses dispersed beneath the trees, rather than a sterile suburb. He drained his coffee mug and put it onto his desk alongside two other dirty ones.

'We didn't turn our backs on him,' said Nalin. 'At least, I didn't. He threw *me* out.'

'I didn't give you the whole story last week,' George said. 'I told him I was a queer. We were in the middle of a row. I expected him to reject me there and then. Perhaps I wanted him to. But he didn't. He was upset – not angry – upset. It made me feel sorry.'

He stared bleakly at Nalin, with his eyes looking straight at him but his face turned downwards.

'I *am* queer. I never meant it to come out the way it did, all the same.'

Nalin went over, stood in front of George and put a hand on each of George's shoulders. He gripped him firmly and pulled him to and fro like a rugby player shaking a team mate who has just scored a try. 'Why do you think I left you on your own with Tim?'

George grinned and partially raised his hands towards his

face as though about to hide behind them.

Nalin released his grip and gave George a playful push. 'I got it right then!'

He sat down on the end of the bed.

'So, what are we going to do about Dad?'

'We'll have to sort things out between you and him for a start,' George said. 'Tell him about Angela. He'll accept it now. He'll be relieved. He'll think anything's better than you being queer as well as me.'

Nalin still had some coffee in his mug. He sipped at it. Looking out of the window, he said, 'We've split up.'

'You didn't tell me.'

'No.'

Nalin thought for a few minutes before pointing out the obvious problem: 'Not very convincing, is it? "Hello, Dad, I've come to tell you I'm not a poof. I've actually split up with a girlfriend you never knew about."' He glanced at his brother, then dropped his eyes and added, 'When I find somebody new I shan't be keeping it secret from Mum and Dad but not until I'm sure about it. There's somebody I fancy but I've hardly got to know. I don't want them gloating if it doesn't work out.'

George picked up the dirty coffee mugs, carried them to the wash basin and rinsed them under the hot tap. A vaguely musty smell rose up as he did. 'It had better be me that talks to Dad again first,' he decided aloud.

He balanced the inverted mugs on the side of the basin to drain.

'Anyway,' he said, bringing the discussion to an end, 'shuttling back and forth between Cambridge and Manchester doesn't leave much time for socialising… I told Simon we might go round.'

'I'd like to see him.'

They went downstairs, bought a couple of donuts and

consumed them as they walked along Wilbraham Road, licking sugar from their lips. Nobody else was on the street except for an elderly woman coming the other way, on the opposite pavement, with a little white dog doing its best to haul her along. She gave the young men a disapproving look. Neither of them realised that eating in the street was frowned upon. The dog viewed things differently from its owner and she yanked it back when it attempted a dash across the road in pursuit of a piece of donut.

It was Simon who came to the door when they knocked. Mrs G was out shopping and Robin was never at home during pub opening hours.

'I thought you'd turn up. Come in a minute while I get my coat.'

'Where are we going?' asked George.

'I don't know. I thought you would.'

They laughed.

'Why don't we walk round Platt Fields?'

It was pleasant to walk in the cool air under a winter sun, and they chatted amiably about nothing of consequence. Nalin could see that George was more comfortable than he had been for years. There was a stronger bond between them now that the thing that could not be said had been said. They had completed two thirds of a circuit of the park – it did not take long – when they were distracted by the clanging of an ambulance bell from the nearby road.

'Oh, heck, that reminds me,' said George. 'I was supposed to take some stuff to the launderette when we came out.'

The other two laughed.

'What's ambulances got to do with washing?' asked Simon.

George laughed as well. 'Dunno!'

Nalin saw his opportunity to get a few minutes alone with Simon. 'We're nearly at your end of the park, George. Why don't you nip back and put stuff in the launderette while we watch the ducks? We can follow in a couple of minutes and meet you over there.' He pointed along a path that led to the main road where the ambulance had passed. 'We can get the bus into town. Last week you said you'd show me round.'

George set off at a trot and Nalin and Simon went towards the lake in silence. They stayed quiet for another minute or two, standing beside it. Nalin, being used to the more peaceful Cambridge, commented on the steady rumble of the Manchester traffic.

Simon nodded. 'It got me really agitated when I first moved here, until I realised what it was that was bothering me. I don't notice it most of the time now.'

Nalin watched some children throwing bread to the ducks, bobbing about on the black water. He said, 'It's none of my business, but I've been thinking…'

Simon turned enquiringly. His expectant face was unsettling.

Nalin continued diffidently, '…about Cathy.'

He pictured how attractively she had been dressed when he met her at Simon's digs, what a kind face she had, and how delicate and soft her skin looked – the sad sight of her giving Simon a little kiss and getting no response from him.

'You ought to tell her the truth.'

Simon did not seem to be offended. He showed no reaction at all except for a blink and the tiniest nod.

'You must know they changed the law a few weeks ago,' Nalin said. 'You're twenty-one. You're not illegal anymore. You don't need to go on pretending.'

'Only for two men in a locked room,' Simon replied, with a hint of resentment in his voice. 'There was a meeting at the Union. They can still get you in other ways – for having sex with somebody when there are other people in the house and there is no lock on the bedroom door – or even if there is a lock, if it's in a hotel. Just for trying to find somebody…

Tim once told me a man even got taken to court for propositioning, just because he smiled at somebody across a bar.' He pulled his jacket closer around himself and tucked his chin down into the collar. 'Changing the law doesn't change what people think.'

'You won't be happy till you can be yourself. How can you be yourself to yourself, if you are not yourself to everybody else? Tim doesn't care what anybody thinks.'

As soon as he had said it, Nalin realised he should not have brought Tim into the conversation. 'Sorry. It's none of my business.'

Simon picked up a small stone from the gravel path and lobbed it into the water. They watched the ripples spreading out from it.

'I already think of us as friends, so it is your business, sort of.' He threw another stone into the pond. He watched the ripples again and then turned, ready to walk away.

'Sorry,' Nalin said again.

Simon turned back to Nalin. 'We've got a lot in common, you and me. I don't have a partner – you don't have a partner. You must be lonely. That's my business. I care about you.' He thought for a moment. Nalin was not his only lonely friend. 'I care about Cathy, too.'

He started to walk towards the road where they would meet George. Nalin walked beside him.

Simon added, 'Don't be sorry. It's fine what you said. Really.'

47

George was back in Cambridge the following weekend. He had not told Nalin he was going and he had not warned his parents. He just turned up at their house towards the end of Friday evening. As he walked in, he told them, without hesitating, he was back to 'sort things out', thus pre-empting whatever his father might have wanted to get in first. Yet they did not discuss much that evening; they sat mostly in silence and went to bed early.

In the morning, his father absented himself under the pretext of having to look after the shop. 'It's busy on Saturday mornings.' It was mid-afternoon when he came back for a late lunch. He sat at the back of the room behind the dining table, in a shaded corner, and watched George, who was sitting in an armchair across the room reading a newspaper, but seeming to give it little attention. They repeatedly caught each other's gaze for a few seconds at a time, but avoided making longer eye contact.

George's father did not leave the table when he finished his meal. Having wiped his fingers, he sat poking at his empty plate as though pushing an invisible grain of rice from place to place. He half got up, and picked up the plate. Without sitting down properly again, still concentrating on the empty plate, he said, 'I went to see the police again yesterday.'

'Oh?'

'They've decided not to pursue charges. They said the evidence would not be sufficient.' He frowned. 'They thought a court would consider I acted in reasonable self-defence. The policeman said that in his opinion it *was* reasonable self-defence. He said people like that brought trouble on themselves.'

He stood up properly, came round from behind the table and walked towards the kitchen, with the plate in his hand.

'Dad,' George said. He got up and put his hand on his father's shoulder. The old man dropped the plate and gave George a tight hug. Then, embarrassed, he pulled away.

'It's all right,' said George. 'It's not broken.'

He picked up the plate and took it into the kitchen. When he came back, his father had gone into the shop again.

That evening, after Nalin had finished working at the theatre, he and George joined Tim in his room.

'How did you get on with Dad?' Nalin asked.

George inhaled a deep breath. 'He's off the hook,' he said. 'The police called him in.'

George's face expressed relief, but his voice sounded puzzled. Tim thought that he might be guessing at what had made the police drop the charges. He directed his gaze away from the other two, appearing to feign casual disinterest. He tried to suppress a slight smile, but George noticed it.

'What do you mean, "he's off the hook"?' asked Nalin.

'According to him, they just said they'd decided not to pursue charges. My guess is, they gave him a formal warning. He seems to think they're expecting him to behave himself and he just had to sign a form. Anyway, the details don't matter. I'm sure he's not got it wrong. He's in the clear.'

'So, it wasn't him after all,' said Nalin. He raised his hand in front of himself, the elbow bent, his fist partially closed and with a pointed forefinger, like a Roman orator declaring that his audience had a great future before them. 'They must have found something else out.'

'If so, he doesn't know or he hasn't told me,' said George sceptically.

'You still think he did it!'

George was ready to reply but Nalin went on. 'You think our dad would go out and murder somebody.'

'I didn't say that. I said we don't know.'

'All the same…'

Tim interrupted the conversation. 'Stop it, you two. The police aren't taking it any further. That's enough, isn't it?'

The brothers glared at him but having their attention taken away from each other made them relax a little.

'I told you he'd be all right,' said Tim. His voice cracked as he went on. 'Your dad's alive. The police don't think there's a case to answer. Donald's dead. That's it.'

George spoke again, calmer than he had been, but still tense. 'If Nalin will let me say what I wanted to, I'm not blaming Dad. Taking a swing was only natural in his mind. He was provoked.'

He looked firmly at Nalin, to block him from breaking in. 'Dad did hit Donald. He told us.'

'Forget history,' Tim said. 'It's what you're going to do now that matters.'

George gave him a penetrating look. 'Something's saved him,' he said.

Tim returned a reproachful frown. 'Is that all you talked about? Him and the police?'

'I've been waiting to report something if you'll give me a chance,' Nalin broke in. 'Dad came looking for me at the theatre on Wednesday. He shuffled his feet about and said he might have been too hasty. It made me smile – out of discomfort, I mean, not mockingly. I was cross with what he said but sorry for him at the same time: he said me living with Tim is disgusting but I'm his son and he'll stand by me. "As long as you don't expect my approval," he said. "Live and let live." Then he blinked as though he was waiting for me to answer.'

'Not exactly magnanimous,' said George. 'And it's irrelevant – he's wrong about you anyway.'

Nalin gave a half nod of acknowledgement. 'There was a wicked bit of me that wanted to let him go on believing what he'd got into his head and say, "It's all right, Dad – I won't make you watch!"' The other two chuckled but it was an uncomfortable response rather than a mirthful one. 'I couldn't, though. I put him right.'

Nalin described how he had explained to his father about his secret meetings with Angela.

'When I told him I'd stopped seeing her, I could see his face brighten up. I told him I wasn't going to agree to an arranged marriage all the same and he didn't say a word. I dropped a hint that there might be somebody else – only a hint but it was clear enough. He just looked blank. I don't think he's going to make an issue of it anymore.'

'He never comes out with anything directly,' George said. He paused. 'It's only by luck I didn't mess it up again by saying the wrong thing. He didn't tell me he'd talked to you.'

Nalin got up and chose an apple from a bowl on the desk. He took a bite and then grinned, saying, 'He still doesn't know about you two, then.'

Tim chuckled. 'What do you mean, "us two"?'

George showed no obvious emotion.

Turning to Tim, Nalin replied, 'I've never seen you this head-over-heels before. Every time you look at George you're like a little boy, gazing at a cuddly teddy bear he just got for his birthday. And George – your eyes light up like Blackpool Illuminations.'

George and Tim gave bashful smiles as Nalin said, joyously, 'You're in love!'

With a satisfied grin, he added, 'Dad's going to have to get used to it.'

48

The telephone rang in the Gupta's house and Mrs Gupta picked up the receiver.

'Who is it?' she asked. There was hostility in Mrs Gupta's voice. The other end of the line said, 'Tell Nalin it's Cathy. I know one of his friends at Manchester University.'

'I'll have to see if I can find him.'

A couple of minutes later, Nalin came to the telephone. Mrs Gupta hovered on the other side of the kitchen door. Nalin's pulse raced.

Cathy said, 'I asked George if there was a way of contacting you and he said you've moved back home.'

'Yes.'

'He gave me the number. I hope you don't mind.'

'Not at all.'

Nalin had not been able to contact Cathy since they had met at Mrs G's.

He had asked George to find out her telephone number, but to no avail, because there was no telephone in her digs. George had offered to get Simon to pass on a message, but Nalin had turned the idea down.

He avoided saying anything that might be interpreted as intimate because he could see his mother's slippered foot through the slightly open kitchen door. Her interest in a phone call to him from a woman had been heightened, no doubt, by the hints that he had been dropping. His obtuse reply was a coded message that Cathy ought to be able to work out:

'I'm settling back in nicely, thanks.'

Cathy took only a moment to respond. She lowered her voice and said, 'I'll come back to the box at ten-fifteen.' She gave him the number of the one she was calling from. She repeated it and said goodbye.

Nalin said, 'All right,' and they both rang off.

His mother's slipper disappeared from view as she moved away quietly, further into the kitchen. She was always early to bed and would be well out of the way by ten-fifteen. His father, obsessed with the business, cashed up every day when the shop closed, and went around re-stocking shelves. He should not be coming through until a bit later than ten-fifteen, but it would be close. The call to Cathy would have to be precisely timed.

He went into the kitchen to help his mother with final household chores, in order to speed up her departure. It was a mistake. The men normally stayed out of the kitchen, leaving her to her own territory, and she seemed to know his apparent filial concern was a pretence. Instead of hastening her departure, it delayed it, as she hung around in case he was mustering the courage to tell her something. It was ten past ten by the time she climbed slowly upstairs. Nalin listened as she finished in the bathroom, returned to her bedroom and closed the door. He felt oppressed by her constant surveillance – he always had done.

Only one more minute passed before the time reached ten-fifteen. Nalin hoped his mother could not hear him making the call in the hallway. The ringing tone sounded for only a few seconds before Cathy answered it.

'You've managed to get me,' she said. 'I was worried there might be somebody in the box but we've struck lucky. I don't know how much your mother knows about you, so it seemed better not to talk earlier.'

Nalin did not have a chance to ask what she meant because Cathy continued, 'It's my twenty-first birthday in June.

Simon's coming. I thought it would be nice if you came with him, you two being special friends.' There was an odd inflection in the way she said it but again she paused too briefly for Nalin to say anything before she added, 'I've invited lots of people from Manchester and friends from home but he doesn't know most of them. It would be nice if you could come.'

'I won't be in the way? Simon's your friend, not me.'

'I wouldn't ask if I didn't mean it. I'm happy to see you together.'

Nalin guessed at a misinterpretation of the facts by Cathy after finding him having breakfast with Simon… his 'special friend'. He wanted to put her right – he wanted to tell her how much she appealed to him – but it was not the moment for it. Perhaps if he went to the party…

'Thanks,' he said. 'I'd like to take up the invitation.' He heard the door to the shop creak as his father opened it. 'Dad's coming.'

'Come to Manchester the night before. You can travel with the others. I'll see you then.'

As Nalin's father came through from the shop, Nalin was putting the receiver back on the hook. If it aroused the old man's curiosity, he did not show it.

49

It was Sunday morning and Cathy arrived to collect Simon from his digs so that they could go together, as usual, to a church service with the Christian Union. Normally they chatted only for a minute or two while Simon put his shoes on, but on this occasion he kept finding extra things he had to do. Mrs G had gone to see her sister and so he cleared the breakfast things away himself. Then he took the cloth off the table and shook it outside the front door. He came in and folded it with slow, careful actions, realigning the creases Mrs G had ironed into it. When he was satisfied it was neat enough, he laid it inside the top drawer of the sideboard. He noticed the drawer did not close easily, pulled it out again and peered at it, rubbing his finger against the top edge.

'Come on,' said Cathy. 'We'll be late.'

'Coming,' said Simon, still fiddling with the drawer.

Cathy sighed. Simon pushed the drawer in, fetched his shoes from the hall and started putting them on. After he had laced up the first, he got up, with one shoe still unfastened, to put some more coal on the fire. Replacing the fireguard, he stepped on one end of the loose shoe lace, pulling it tight and making it much longer than the other end. He sat on the rug in front of the fire, pulled some of the lengthened end back through the eyehole in his shoe and worked the excess along, eyehole by eyehole, until he could extend the shorter one, before tying a neat bow. He fetched his coat from the hall and fiddled about brushing off particles of dust before he put it on. He pulled a solitary glove out of his coat pocket and looked around for the other one. Not finding it, he decided to tuck the one he was holding behind the clock on the mantelpiece.

Cathy led the way to the front door. As she opened it to step out, Simon said, 'Actually, is it all right if we don't go this morning?'

Cathy looked over her shoulder at him. 'Are you all right?'

'There's something I have to tell you.'

'You're not in trouble with the police?' There was no hint of censoriousness in her voice – only concern.

They came back in and sat down, one in each of the armchairs on either side of the fire. Cathy had half-expected Simon to run into trouble with the law for a long time. She waited for his answer.

Simon watched the smoke rising from the newly stoked fire, took his time preparing his words, and said, 'When we were on the train coming back from visiting my parents, I said I couldn't marry you…'

'If that really is the only thing worrying you, Simon… Once I'd had time to think, I realised it was for the best.'

'Are you sure?' asked Simon.

'Yes. Unless… No, honestly – it's all right. We're better off just being friends.'

'I meant it when I told you it wasn't anything about you.'

Cathy gave him a gentle, encouraging look. 'I've come to understand that.'

'I can't get married. I can't help it.'

A few flames were beginning to flit over the coals, suddenly springing up and then dying. Cathy watched them struggling to survive in the midst of the surrounding smoke, failing to burst into glory – to declare themselves victorious and proud to face the world.

'I keep falling in love with men,' said Simon.

Cathy smiled.

'Bless you, Simon. I've already got that worked out. I didn't like to say anything.'

Simon stared at Cathy and just said, 'Oh.'

'It seemed easier to let things drift along,' Cathy said. 'There was this awful thing in the back of my mind that I might have got it wrong. I kept thinking of the damage it would do if I came out with it and all the time there was something else troubling you.'

They sat looking at one another in silence for a while before Simon said, 'Nobody else knows… except Nalin.'

'I thought it must be him.'

For a few seconds, Simon did not seem to understand what Cathy meant. Then he pulled his head back slightly in realisation, immediately dipping it down again with embarrassment.

'When I found him with you at breakfast,' she continued, 'after he stayed for the night…'

She noticed Simon's expression. 'Oh, Simon. I'm sorry. Have I got it wrong?'

'He's really companionable but he's not…' Simon hesitated before he used the word 'homosexual'. 'He's split up with his girlfriend but that's because it wasn't working out.'

Cathy said, 'You need to find somebody.'

They both fell silent. A tiny jet of gas hissing out of a piece of coal ignited, went out, ignited again. The clock on the mantelpiece over the fire ticked steadily. Its second hand calibrated the relentless progress of time in quanta.

'You need to find someone, too,' said Simon.

'Now I know there really isn't anything between you and Nalin' – Cathy gave Simon a little, conspiratorial smile – 'I must say he is rather nice.'

'No, there really isn't.' He blinked and passed his hand over his face. 'I haven't got anybody at the moment and neither has he.'

He sat staring into the fire gloomily.

'Simon,' Cathy added, 'you're not ashamed are you? I know you can't ignore social attitudes but it's no reason to be ashamed. Are you frightened?'

'I wasn't ashamed to start with; I wasn't all that frightened – just wary about letting people find out… It kept getting harder – knowing you're the worst of the worst in the eyes of everybody around you. It gets to you in the end.'

'There are three stories about people in love in the Bible,' Cathy said. 'Samson was besotted with Delilah and she tricked and destroyed him, which is a bit unfortunate if you're looking for role models in the scriptures. To me, the other two are about true love – Ruth and Naomi, and David and Jonathan.'

Simon remembered sitting with Cathy, listening to the story of David and Jonathan when he had taken her home for the weekend. How different might things have been if he had known then that she saw the story the way he did.

'I've stopped being scared. I'm angry more than fearful. I'm so angry with how society has treated us – so angry with the police, the government, the churches –'

Cathy held a clenched fist in the air. 'Yes!'

Simon had never seen her like this. She had always seemed so demure.

'Fight, Simon – fight like the devil. Oh dear. Me, a respectable Baptist.' She laughed. 'We're not supposed to be on his side!'

'Like the devil?' asked Simon, softly. 'Or the Devil's Disciple?'

'George Bernard Shaw. Did you read it at school as well?' Cathy asked.

'Like the Devil's Disciple,' Simon repeated with a resolute edge to his voice, looking Cathy straight in the eyes.

50

Lena, Harold, Melanie and Ruth went to the coast for a short holiday at Whitsuntide. It was the first time they had done anything as a foursome, apart from having Sunday dinner together a couple of times a month. They stood beside the harbour in Whitby, watching fishermen busy in their boats.

'Let's get some candy floss,' said Lena. 'Or would you rather have shrimps?'

'Candy floss!' Ruth replied. 'Like the little girl's got over there. It's nearly as big as she is!'

They went along the street towards the pier. It was about half-tide. Strands of seaweed hung from the harbour walls, their ends swaying in the gently rising and falling water. The air was filled with the smell of the sea, and gulls were wheeling and calling.

The candy floss stall was a few yards short of the pier. They watched the magical spinning of their purchases in the machine.

'I think the last time I ate candy floss was when I was the age of that little girl Ruth pointed out,' Harold said.

'No, it wasn't,' Melanie said. 'You used to eat bits of mine!'

'I suppose I did, now you remind me.'

He reached over and stole a little piece of Melanie's candy floss.

'People don't change,' Melanie joked.

They walked the length of the pier. For a few minutes they watched some boys fishing for mackerel, patiently waiting for a bite, seated with their legs perilously dangling over the edge, high above the water, and their fishing lines trailed between their fingers. Then the four of them turned back onto the promenade and descended to the beach. It was not busy, and they found a place to themselves. The sand was warm from the spring sunshine.

'Shall we go for a paddle?' Melanie said.

They were wearing their bathing costumes under their other clothes, which they pulled off and piled onto a towel. They padded across the firmer sand below the high-tide mark and down to the edge of the surf. The sea was not rough, and they watched the waves rolling towards them. One wave broke over another. Water surged up the beach and washed over their feet.

'Aiyee!' shouted Ruth. 'It's cold.'

'You'll get used to it,' said Lena.

'Maybe, but I'm not going in above my knees.'

As she spoke, Harold dashed forward, sending up a shower of spray. When he was beyond the closest waves and more than waist-deep, he dived right through a big one that was breaking towards him and reappeared swimming strongly beyond it.

'Oh my goodness,' said Melanie.

He did not swim much further before turning towards the shore. He splashed out of the water and took Lena's hand.

'Come on.'

The two of them repeated the round trip out beyond the breaking waves and back.

'You're right,' Harold said to Ruth. 'It's cold.'

They trotted up the beach, dried their bodies and sat on the sand, hugging themselves, with their towels draped over their shoulders.

'We'll soon warm up in the sun.'

They sat in silence for a while, watching a ship steaming past almost at the horizon. After a few minutes they lay back on the sand. The wind from the sea was cool but it blew gently.

Lying close to the ground, the family – for they were now a family – felt only the warmth of the sun. Harold sat up.

'I just want you to know Melanie… Ruth… I've given it a lot of thought.'

A couple of children came past, close by. He watched them run onto the firmer sand and start to fill their buckets with it.

'People do change. Even if their principles don't change, it doesn't mean the rules they build out of them are immutable. I'm glad things have come out the way they have. I'm just sorry about the time it's taken me to understand. It is love that matters, not who loves who.'

Lena and Melanie turned their heads to look at each other and smiled. Then Melanie turned her smile towards her father, who was looking at her, and said, very softly, 'Yes.'

All four of them got up. Cloaking themselves in their towels to maintain decency, they changed into their dry clothes. They walked up the beach and along the street beside the harbour. The tide had risen a little higher. The swing bridge was open, and they watched a boat come through. Once the bridge had swung back, they crossed it into the old town and found a fish and chip shop.

They had eaten the food and were finishing their cups of tea when Harold said, 'Do you remember Peter Salt?'

'I wonder what happened to him,' Lena replied. 'He just disappeared.'

Harold put down his empty cup and rearranged the teaspoon beside it. He thought about the way his attitudes were changing and wondered if the same was happening to other people. 'Perhaps things will get better. I hope they will.'

51

It was as Cathy had said when she had spoken to Nalin on the telephone: her party was thronging with people that neither Simon nor Nalin had ever met. They started mingling with them but inevitably, after a while, they ended up talking to each other in a corner of the spacious living room. There were still enough people chatting loudly, over the sound of the Rolling Stones coming from the radiogram, for their conversation to go unnoticed. Most of the party had migrated to the kitchen.

'You must feel a bit out of it, being the only Indian,' said Simon.

'I'm used to it. You're never really on the inside of a party anyway, if nearly all the others are strangers.' Nalin looked at his friend. 'It doesn't seem to matter at this one though.' He smiled.

Another guest wandered by, on his way from the conservatory to join the crowd in the kitchen. Nalin waited for him to pass.

'Don't *you* feel out of it, never being yourself?'

'Of course I feel out of it. I *am* out of it.'

'You should at least tell the truth to the people most likely to get hurt if you don't.' There was a sharp edge in Nalin's voice.

They could see Cathy, leaning against the fridge in the kitchen, in conversation with two local friends. Nalin looked towards her pointedly.

Simon nodded and blinked. 'I've told her.'

Nalin smiled.

'Well, actually,' Simon went on, 'I did tell her but she said she already knew.'

Somebody in the conservatory dropped a glass. There was a brief silence and then a commotion of laughter. The woman who had dropped it came through for a dustpan and cloth and went back to clear up the pieces. The background hubbub returned to its former level.

'It was such a relief, knowing she wasn't expecting anything from me.' Simon brought a waver in his voice under control. 'So I've got two friends who don't think worse of me for it. Cathy as well as you.'

'And plenty more people if only you could wake up to the reality. The ones who reject you aren't your friends. They're the ones with a problem, not you. Let them go. Be proud to be different. If enough of you were, you could change things.'

'I'm working on that,' Simon said, in such an understated tone of voice that Nalin did not register its significance.

Nalin's face took on a puckish smirk. 'What about him over there? He keeps looking at you. I'm sure he wants to be introduced.'

'Nalin!'

'Come on.'

Nalin pulled Simon up by the hand from his chair and went over to the stranger. 'Hello,' he said. 'We're friends of Cathy's from Manchester. At least, Simon is. I'm a sort of hanger-on from Cambridge.'

The stranger started straight into a conversation with Simon. Nalin slipped away and left them to it.

Cathy came through from the kitchen and noticed that Nalin was on his own.

'Nalin, this is all very embarrassing but I've got an apology to make.'

She led Nalin out through the conservatory and into the

garden. It was a pleasant summer evening, but it was cooling down and the light was fading. They stood under a pergola laden with flowering honeysuckle. There was barely any breeze and the sweet scent hung in the air. Nobody else was outside. Someone had changed the record and turned the volume down on the radiogram, so there was only the distant sound of chattering voices from inside the house.

'Has Simon told you? I hope not. It ought to come from me. When I first met you I thought you and him were… lovers, I suppose the word is.'

She chuckled.

'Isn't it awful of me. I do hope you're not offended. I don't see men loving each other as terribly wrong, but I don't imagine you want people thinking it of *you* all the same.'

Nalin gave Cathy a kindly smile.

'When he introduced us, I was worried you were expecting him to marry you,' he said. 'I was worried he might actually do it. It would have messed both of your lives up. He's got to accept the way he is.'

'Golly. We seem to share the same views. You probably expected me to be old-fashioned when it comes to family relationships – no sex before marriage, no mixed marriages… I've got to admit I was old-fashioned when I was younger – more old-fashioned than my parents – they're very easy-going. It's funny how you rebel against your parents and then end up agreeing with them. The liberal-minded bit of my inheritance fought back. Your parents must be dead against anything that breaks conventions, aren't they?'

'I used to think they'd go into mental decline if they found out a member of the family had once tasted the corner of an Oxo cube. It's not clear to me what their attitudes are now. You never know people's true feelings. When it comes to moral opinions, most people let the world think they conform to expectations, whatever they really believe. It all hinges on the environment they find themselves in.'

Nalin pulled a flower from the honeysuckle and gave it to Cathy.

'I thought you'd got the wrong idea about me and Simon at first when you telephoned to invite me. Then, when you sent me that letter a week or two after, I realised I'd been wrong and that calling me Simon's friend was just an excuse to get me here. With the way things have gone between us since, I don't have any worries now.'

'Well, you know now. I did have the wrong idea when I invited you. To be honest, I fancied you like anything, but I would never have broken up your relationship with Simon, if there'd been one. As soon as I found out there was nothing like that and you were available…'

She smelled the honeysuckle flower and then, taking the lapel of Nalin's jacket in one hand, she pushed the flower into the button hole.

'Come and say hello to Mum and Dad. They're dying to meet you.' She took his hand, and they turned to go back into the house to find Cathy's parents. 'They don't know about Simon, by the way. I'm sure it wouldn't matter to them. But it's not for us to let on. That's for Simon to decide.'

They lingered a little longer beneath the honeysuckle. Nalin took hold of a trailing stem gently. Cathy watched him studying the flower that hung from it.

'Simon says he's going to Cambridge with George at the end of term for a party,' she said. 'Their friend Tim's staying on in college for a few days so that they can have a little get-together. I imagine you'll go to it, being Simon's friend and George's brother?'

'I wouldn't call it a party – it will only be us,' Nalin said. He thought for a moment. 'Will you come?'

'Why do you think I asked you about it? I'll come as long as Simon does.'

Nalin's downward-tilted face was hard to read in the failing light, but he looked disgruntled.

'Nalin, don't look like that. I don't mean I want to come because Simon will be there. You ought to know by now it's got to be you I want to come to see. He's an ideal chaperone if anybody is. What would your parents think if I travelled down by myself? I know my parents wouldn't like it – a young woman on a train on her own – not that they'd admit it.'

'Of course Simon is coming,' Nalin said.

'Perhaps I'll get a chance to meet your parents.'

Nalin leaned forward and kissed Cathy very briefly on the forehead, before they went back inside.

52

On the date of the get-together in Cambridge, Cathy and George arrived without Simon. Nalin was at the station to meet them.

'He promised he'd come. Now he's gone to London saying he might join us later,' Cathy said.

'He'll turn up,' said George.

'That's not what he said. He said he might.'

It had been arranged that Cathy would stay with one of Nalin's female work colleagues who more usually put up visiting performers for a night or two.

'We can take your things round to Abigail's later on,' Nalin said. 'Let's go over to Tim's room for now and drop George's stuff off.'

Once they were there, Tim closed the door behind them and hugged George, before giving him a kiss. Cathy had never seen two men kiss before; she did not have time to consider how she felt about it. She and Nalin had not greeted each other properly at the station and he took the opportunity now to hug and kiss her.

Tim provided some cakes from Fitzbillies' shop. 'To keep us going,' he said.

They sat down and began eating them.

Nalin wiped a dollop of cream from the end of Cathy's nose and said, 'I did wonder myself whether Simon would come.'

'It's as though he's going backwards,' Cathy replied. 'I thought he was making progress and then he told me last night he was going to London. He says he'll come on the train this evening as long as it isn't too late. The thing is, he won't.'

She seemed so certain about it that the others lost interest in their cakes and gave her their full attention.

'I thought he was getting – well – a bit over the top, if anything. Politically, I mean. What he calls "Gay Liberation". He's got mixed up with this campaigning group. I'm not against them. I wouldn't rule out going on a demonstration with them if it came to it, but they're very confrontational. I thought it was only a matter of time before he was out in the street waving a flag. Then, all of a sudden, he's been dragged into evangelism! I didn't even know until last night, when he told me he couldn't travel with me this morning, because he's going to an evangelist rally. You can't get further from liberation than that.'

She peered at her cake as though it might hold the solution to her distress. 'They'll tell him they can cure him with prayers.'

'That's not going to work,' said George.

'I know it isn't. That's why it matters,' said Cathy.

'He's not ill,' said Nalin.

'As I said, that's why it matters.'

'Simon always had a fixation about conforming to social norms,' Tim chimed in. 'That's what got him into the mess he's been in. But when he makes a decision, he's more bloody-minded than he lets on, whether it's a decision that complies with everybody else's expectations or not. If he's started fighting for justice, evangelists aren't going to drag him down. They lost their chance the day he signed up with the Gay Liberation Squad.'

'That's it. Gay Liberation Squad,' said Cathy. 'I forgot the "Squad" bit.'

'From what I've heard,' Tim began with a gleeful smile, 'they're more evangelical than the evangelicals. They won't let him apostatise now they've got him!'

There was nothing the others could say to follow that. They fell quiet, licking and nibbling until they had finished their cream cakes.

They decided they would eat out at a Chinese restaurant in the evening and then return to Tim's room for an hour or two before they went to their different lodgings for the night. Cathy would go to Abigail's, Nalin would stay with his parents and George would spend the night with Tim. If Simon did turn up, Abigail had a room for him, too.

It left a gap in the afternoon.

'Have you ever seen King's College Chapel?' Tim asked Cathy.

'I've never been to Cambridge before,' she replied.

'Would you believe George's never been inside?' Tim said.

'Nobody visits the tourist attractions where they live,' George said. 'I'm not into religion anyway.'

'Never mind about religion,' said Tim. 'It's just an amazing building. You've got to see it. Why don't we go this afternoon?'

George tilted his head and raised an eyebrow in assent, but Cathy looked at Nalin, who appeared to be uncomfortable.

'There's a complication,' he said.

The others waited for him to continue.

'Cathy wants to meet my parents and I've told them she's coming.' His face was almost one of guilt – the look of somebody confessing to a mistake with embarrassing consequences. 'It never crossed my mind they'd actually agree to it.'

George said his father must have a hidden motive, probably to humiliate Cathy and bring shame on Nalin.

Nalin said, 'We'd better leave it. I shouldn't have said anything to them. If they get the impression we're really serious about each other they'll only get into a flap.'

He realised at once that he might have spoken out of turn. He did not know whether Cathy was as serious about him as he was about her. He looked at her for a moment and then half whispered, 'That is, I mean – I don't mean…' He turned to George and said, 'George's right. It's a stupid idea. Let's all go to King's College.'

'I'm not some delicate, rare species. You don't have to screen me from what your parents might think,' Cathy said, getting up and taking hold of Nalin's hand. 'Come on.' Turning to the others she said, 'We'll meet you at King's College or, if it's too late, we'll see you back here.'

It happened that the organist was practising for a forthcoming service in King's College Chapel. George had never heard an organ live and in full cry before, and he and Tim stood listening to it for a while. By the time they had completed their visit, Cathy and Nalin still had not turned up, and so they crossed the road to a café. Tim thought the delay must mean they were getting on well. George remarked that Cathy was capable of being more combative than her normally calm manner suggested, and it was more likely that they were tangled up in a row.

'We might as well walk back,' Tim said when they had finished their coffees.

As they stepped out of the café, Cathy and Nalin were coming along the street.

'Do you want to go back across to the chapel?' Tim asked.

'It doesn't matter. There'll be another time,' Cathy said.

'How did you get on?' Tim asked, looking first at Cathy, then at Nalin.

Nalin seemed unwilling to comment but Cathy answered. 'We did fine. I told you all not to be so pessimistic.'

'They didn't exactly embrace you into the family,' said Nalin.

'Oh, come on. Nobody's parents would. Not just like that. They've never met me before.'

'They were ready to hitch me to somebody *I'd* never met.'

'Anyway. They didn't throw me out.'

The four of them slowed their pace. The expressions on George's face and Tim's as they exchanged glances both implied the thought *I told you so*, but their interpretations of the conversation they had just heard were probably in contradiction. Then George's expression became more hopeful.

He said, 'Do you think they might get used to you two?' He stopped, causing the others almost to collide with him. '... And to me and Tim?'

All four of them joined hands and sauntered on, spanning the pavement and oblivious to the people coming the other way who were forced to step into the road to get by.

It was still a bit early to eat and so they returned to Tim's room, agreeing they would go out at about seven-thirty. They were happy in each other's company, but they were tired and the conversation often lapsed into a comfortable silence.

When it was close to seven-thirty, Tim asked, 'Have you seen colour TV yet?'

'Only in shop windows,' George replied.

'We've just got one in the common room,' said Tim. 'Shall we go and watch *Newsroom* on BBC2 before we go out?'

There were about a dozen other students watching the television, all sitting towards the far side of the room. Tim greeted two who looked round but the rest were wrapped up in the news, which had just started. The new arrivals found a group of chairs slightly separate from the people already there, turned them towards the TV and sat down on them – not out of aloofness, it was just where the empty chairs were. Huge crowds were being shown on the screen, gathering in Hyde Park for a rock concert.

'I didn't know that was on,' Cathy said.

'Would you have wanted to go?' Tim asked. 'We could have done.'

‘It’s not my thing, trooping along with half-a-million people. Coming here is much nicer.’

‘Perhaps that’s where Simon’s gone,’ George said. ‘Perhaps he isn’t at a Christian rally at all.’

‘George!’ Cathy replied. ‘Simon wouldn’t make that sort of thing up.’

The presenter moved on to the last item in the programme. ‘There was confusion this afternoon at a somewhat smaller event – a Christian rally in North London where prayers were disrupted by shouts of “Thou shalt love thy neighbour” from hecklers. Six men were arrested in front of the entrance to the building for behaviour likely to cause a breach of the peace, after allegedly kissing each other in public.’

The screen showed a group of men being led away by the police, their backs to the camera. ‘We understand they have all been released without charge after questioning.’ While he was speaking the camera panned in on two of the men being led away, one with hair almost the colour of turmeric.

‘It can’t really be that bright,’ one of the students said. Even as he spoke, the two men began to swivel round, and Nalin recognised who it was. Cathy and Tim already had. The men on the television faced the camera directly, turned their heads to look into each other’s eyes, pouting their lips, then turned to the camera again and, in unison, blew kisses to the viewers.

Cathy jumped up. ‘Simon!’

One of the other students in the room had noticed someone coming in through the door. ‘It’s him!’ he shouted.

Almost everyone got up and turned to look at Simon, who, taken by surprise at the reaction to his entrance, stopped just inside the doorway. The voices of some of the cheering students carried a hint of a jeer, but it was the kind that is amused rather than outright derogatory. Most of them were clearly in awe of the man who had staged such a daring challenge to respectability and authority. Simon smiled the smile of someone who is pleased and flattered but not sure that he deserves adulation.

Tim felt suddenly uncomfortable, fearing that the apparent solidarity with Simon might change to a mocking attack. 'Come on,' he said, and he led Nalin, Cathy, Tim and Simon out of the door and back to his room.

Nobody was sure what to say. They were all so excited, it was hard to know where to begin.

'How did you feel when you got arrested?' Tim asked. 'How did they treat you?'

'It was scary if I'm honest, but it made a big difference being one in a team with a mission, so to speak. We were treated all right, I suppose.'

'You were all let off – they said on the news,' George said.

'They got that wrong. Most of us were let off but not the ones who kissed each other. They'll be up in court. I fooled around on the steps outside for the benefit of the cameras, but I didn't actually kiss anybody. Funny thing is, I was one of the ones who shouted in the meeting and I got away with that. But it's still illegal to do anything the least affectionate outside a locked room.

'The police and the courts aren't going to change their attitudes. You'll see, there'll be an increase in people getting convicted, not a decrease. I'm going to fight for better treatment, and I'll push to the limit of what we can get away with. It's not that clear what the limit is, but I intend to go as close as I dare without crossing it.'

They were all quiet for a minute or two.

Then Cathy said to Simon, 'You've come out of your shell!'

Simon looked thoughtful. 'Not like a snail, though. Like a chicken.'

The others laughed.

'Some chicken!' said Tim.

'We all start out in a shell,' Simon said. 'Most people don't even notice they're in one. They become accommodated to it – inhabit their circumscribed little lives. It's safe inside a shell.' Apprehensively, he added, 'If you break out of it you can't go back – you can't put it back together.'

'But you're free,' said Nalin.

Simon relaxed and gave a broad smile. The flexing of his whole body expressed jubilation.

'You're free.'